B's

P9-CQA-525

"Gabe! Come over," the matchmakers yelled. "We've figured out the perfect man for Katie to marry so you'll be off the hook."

"There's a rancher with four children. He needs a mother for them. Katie—"

"No! She's already raised her brothers and sisters." Gabe remembered Katie's face when he'd asked if she'd gone to college. His heart ached for her lost dreams.

"There's the minister. Katie would make an excellent minister's wife," Florence said.

"No, I don't want—" Gabe stopped, frustrated. "Damn! Isn't there someone who would let Katie be Katie? Who would help her? She deserves the best!"

"Well, of course she does," Edith said. "I told them that, but they argued with me."

He nodded eagerly at Edith. "Yeah? Who did you think would do for Katie?" He wasn't going to marry Katie off to just anyone.

"Why, Gabe, dear, the perfect man is you."

Dear Reader,

It's another wonderful month at Harlequin American Romance, the line dedicated to bringing you stories of heart, home and happiness! Just look what we have in store for you....

Author extraordinaire Cathy Gillen Thacker continues her fabulous series THE LOCKHARTS OF TEXAS with *The Bride Said, "Finally!"* Cathy will have more Lockhart books out in February and April 2001, as well as a special McCabe family saga in March 2001.

You've been wanting more books in the TOTS FOR TEXANS series, and author Judy Christenberry has delivered! *The $10,000,000 Texas Wedding* is the not-to-be-missed continuation of these beloved stories set in Cactus, Texas. You just know there's plenty of romance afoot when a bachelor will lose his huge inheritance should he fail to marry the woman he once let get away.

Rounding out the month are two fabulous stories by two authors making their Harlequin American Romance debut. Neesa Hart brings us the humorous *Who Gets To Marry Max?* and Victoria Chancellor will wow you with *The Bachelor Project.*

Wishing you happy reading!

Melissa Jeglinski
Associate Senior Editor

The
$10,000,000
Texas Wedding

JUDY CHRISTENBERRY

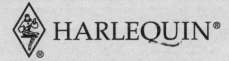

HARLEQUIN®

TORONTO • NEW YORK • LONDON
AMSTERDAM • PARIS • SYDNEY • HAMBURG
STOCKHOLM • ATHENS • TOKYO • MILAN • MADRID
PRAGUE • WARSAW • BUDAPEST • AUCKLAND

ISBN 0-373-16842-X

THE $10,000,000 TEXAS WEDDING

ABOUT THE AUTHOR

Judy Christenberry has been writing romances for fifteen years because she loves happy endings as much as her readers. Judy quit teaching French recently and now devotes her time to writing. She hopes readers have as much fun reading her stories as she does writing them. She spends her spare time reading, watching her favorite sports teams and keeping track of her two daughters. Judy's a native Texan, but now lives in Arizona.

Books by Judy Christenberry

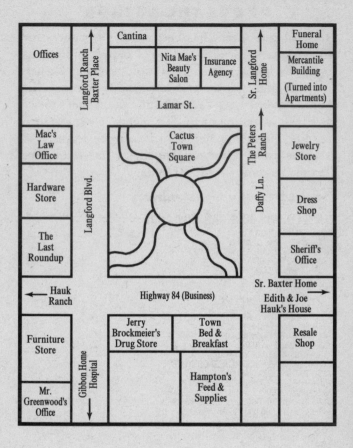

Chapter One

Cactus, Texas.

Gabe Dawson carefully pulled into a parking space on the town square. He didn't want to have a wreck on his first day back in town. With memories pouring into his head, he feared he might be too distracted to drive.

He'd grown up here, learning about life, sharing, hunting, camping, riding with his friends. Falling in love for the first time. Katie.

"Gabe!"

The man standing by his car door waited for him to acknowledge his presence. Gabe opened the door and got out. "Mac Gibbons!" he replied, grabbing one of his best childhood friends into a bear hug. "How did you know I was here?"

"I'd been to see Cal. Your new Mercedes caught my eye. Nice car."

"Yeah, thanks." The car was a result of his recent success. "I was on my way to see you."

"About your grandmother's will?"

Gabe nodded.

Mac reached out and squeezed Gabe's shoulder in silent sympathy. "Come on, let's get it over with. Then we can visit."

Mac Gibbons knew Gabriel Dawson was in for a shock. He decided it would be better not to procrastinate. He hoped Gabe would take some time to think, not make a quick decision.

He led his old friend into his offices. After introducing him to his secretary, an efficient middle-aged woman, he took him down the hall, stopping at the first door.

"Alex, let me introduce an old friend, Gabe Dawson. Alexandra Langford is my partner."

"Langford?" Gabe repeated, a question in his voice.

Mac nodded. "And Tuck's wife."

Gabe smiled. "Tuck always was a lucky man. But I'll admit, I never thought he'd marry."

Mac chuckled. "One look at Alex, and he was a goner."

Alexandra gave her partner a knowing look. "You don't have room to talk, Mac."

"Yeah," he agreed with a contented sigh.

"You remarried?" Gabe asked, astounded. He'd been around when Mac had lived in Dallas. He knew how badly his friend had been hurt.

"He married and is a daddy twice over," Alex added.

Mac's grin only widened. "Never mind that. We'll catch up later. First, we've got some business to conduct."

He led his friend into his office and shut the door.

Before sitting down, he pulled a legal file from his file cabinet. "Your grandmother changed her will last year."

Gabe's head snapped up. "Do you mean I'm not the heir?"

It wasn't that he needed his grandmother's estate. As an attorney with a large firm in Dallas, he earned a more-than-healthy salary. Then he'd taken a risk on a personal injury case and had won big. Big enough that he'd never have to work again.

But he'd loved his grandmother. He wouldn't want to think he'd disappointed her.

"You're still the heir," Mac assured him, "if you meet certain conditions."

"Certain conditions?" Foreboding filled Gabe. His grandmother had fussed about his lifestyle. Surely she hadn't—

"You know how amazed you were that Tuck and I were both married?"

Gabe stared at his friend. What did their marriages have to do with anything? "Well, yeah, Tuck was determined never to marry and you, well, I was there when you went through your divorce. I remember how bitter and hurt you were."

Mac nodded. "Spence and Cal are married, too," he added, naming two other friends. "It seems our mothers were frustrated that we hadn't married, any of us, and made a bet to see who would get the first grandbaby. They were so successful, they inspired a lot of other mothers…and grandmothers."

"Are you telling me Gran changed her will to—to force me to marry?"

Mac nodded. "Yeah. I tried to talk her out of it, but you know how hardheaded she was." He lifted several papers and passed them to Gabe before sitting down behind his desk. "You might as well read it yourself."

Gabe took the will, his brows furrowing. He couldn't believe Gran would try to force his hand. He'd been engaged once, but Gran hadn't seemed too pleased with his choice. So why would she try to rush him into something?

He quickly read the papers, noting the requirement that he return to Cactus for one year. Outrageous, but not impossible. It would take him that long to sell her house. In the meantime, he would live there.

But it was the last requirement that had him leaping to his feet. "Marry Katherine? Was she crazy? Katie married over eight years ago. This is insane. When did she write this?"

"About six months ago. Katie is a widow now."

Gabe swallowed. "I can't believe she'd agree to this blackmail."

"I don't know whether she agreed or not. And there is a provision, saving you from that requirement if Katie marries someone else."

"Where is she? I'm going to share a few facts of life with Miss Katherine Peters!" he exclaimed, turning to charge out of the room.

"Katherine Hill. And you'll find her at The

Lemon Drop Shop,'' Mac obligingly told Gabe, a speculative look in his eyes.

''The what?'' Gabe said, coming to an abrupt halt.

''It's a bakery on the other side of the square. That's how she supports herself these days.''

Gabe had avoided seeing Katie when he'd come back to visit his grandmother. His trips had always been brief and far apart. He hadn't even visited the guys very often. He was always too busy.

Gran had come to stay with him at Christmas every year, preferring his bachelor apartment to his parents' pretentious house in one of those neighborhoods in Dallas where the houses were huge and the lots small.

''She must not have been of sound mind when she made the changes,'' Gabe protested.

''I'm afraid you won't be able to prove that,'' Mac assured him.

''Then Katie must have put her up to it. She probably needs the money and thought I'd be easy plucking.'' He paced back to Mac's desk. ''Is she still supporting half her family?''

Mac nodded. ''Most of the kids are grown. Two are still in high school. And then there's her mother.''

''That's what it is. She planned to cash in. Well, she turned me down once. She won't get that chance again.'' This time, when he turned to storm out of Mac's office, his friend didn't say anything to stop him.

Gabe stepped onto the sidewalk and saw the

bright sign across the square. The Lemon Drop Shop. Every letter was lemon yellow on a white background. There were small tables and chairs in front of the store, with lemon-yellow umbrellas to provide shade. It looked clean, fresh, delectable.

He charged across the street, jogging through the square, past the band shell and onto the opposite sidewalk. His mind was whirling with the news he'd received.

But even more upsetting was the intense anticipation that filled him. Katie Peters. No, Katie Hill, a widow. She'd probably be fat and dumpy, desperate for his grandmother's wealth. He prayed she was. He didn't want to see her.

Which didn't explain why he was running.

Anger, that was it. He was angry that she'd swayed his sweet grandmother to act so irrationally.

A bell jangled as he swung open the door to The Lemon Drop Shop, and he wanted to strangle it. But almost no one paid him any attention.

Until he roared her name. "Katie Hill? Where are you?"

KATHERINE HILL WAS DECORATING a large tray of cookies. She enjoyed making the first few as she transformed the pale dough into bright butterflies. But as her back began to ache from bending over the counter, and she repeated the same designs again and again, she wished she were done.

Especially when someone yelled her name.

Startled, her hand jerked and the blue icing

missed its mark. Instead, it shot across the wax paper onto the cookie beside it.

"Damn!" Katherine muttered softly. She took a knife to scrape off the wayward icing. Then she wiped her hands on the big apron she wore and pushed open the door that led into the front room. The friendly smile on her face disappeared, however, when she faced the man standing in the middle of the shop, his hands cocked on his hips.

Gabriel Dawson.

Katherine immediately shut away the memories that wanted to come cascading down through her mind. Another time, another life.

She purposefully swept emotion from her face. "May I help you?"

"Don't act like you don't know me, Katie!" he ordered, his voice a threatening growl.

"Oh, sorry, Gabe. The sun made it hard for me to see you. What are you doing in Cactus?"

"You know what I'm doing here!"

The customers in the shop, those sitting at the small tables and others in line to be waited on, were staring at them. Even the two women who worked for Katherine were frozen.

She didn't know what he was talking about, but she knew she didn't want to discuss it with an audience. "Why don't you find a table outside? I'll bring us some drinks and a snack."

"It won't do you any good to try to sweeten me up. It's not going to work!"

Had the man gone stark raving mad? She hadn't seen him since she'd turned down his marriage proposal ten years ago. Well, that wasn't quite true. She'd occasionally seen him from a distance and hastily run in the opposite direction.

But he hadn't come to visit Mrs. Dawson all that often. For which she'd been grateful.

"I'll be right out," she muttered, avoiding everyone's stare. "Mary, Evelyn, I believe some of our customers are waiting."

The two ladies snapped out of their stupor and began waiting on the customers again, and Katherine returned to the workroom. She didn't look to see whether Gabe had followed her suggestion. If he decided to storm out as abruptly as he'd stormed in, she wouldn't object.

She didn't need any grief from him.

Putting several of the butterfly cookies on a plate, she loaded the plate on a tray and added two glasses of lemonade, along with napkins and straws.

After taking a deep breath, she pushed her way through the swinging door. She paused when she realized Gabe wasn't still standing in the middle of her shop.

"He's outside," Evelyn whispered.

Katherine gave her employee a calm smile and walked to the glass door. One of her male customers immediately sprang to his feet to hold the door open for her. With a quiet thank-you, she stepped outside.

It was spring in Cactus, when a cool breeze kept the air pleasant and everything was still green. In summer it got hot and the grass turned a dingy brown-green.

But Gabriel Dawson didn't look like he was enjoying the season. He glowered at her, standing as she approached the table.

With fourteen years experience as a waitress behind her, Katherine set the two glasses and the plate on the table, then added the napkins and straws. She handed the tray to her brother, Paul, who worked for her in the afternoon.

"Thanks, Paul."

Her words gave her companion pause.

"Paul? Is that you?" Gabe demanded.

When he'd left, Paul had been a seven-year-old who idolized him, following him around whenever he saw him.

"Yeah, Gabe," Paul said with a grin. After a sharp look from Katherine, he added, "I mean, Mr. Dawson."

Gabe glared at her again. "I think Gabe will be just fine, Paul. It's good to see you." He stuck out his hand and Paul took it.

Katherine was proud of her brother. He worked hard for her without complaint. After her shop closed, he returned home and did the chores. Then he attacked his homework with the same fervor.

He would graduate this year as the valedictorian if his grades held up this last semester.

"You're all grown-up," Gabe told her brother, smiling for the first time.

Katherine quickly looked away. That smile had been her world, once upon a time. It hurt too much to see it now.

"Yeah. It's been a long time," Paul returned,

then glanced hurriedly at his sister. "Well, I'd better—I've got things to do. Let me know if I can get you anything."

"Sure. Thanks. Maybe we can visit later."

Paul gave a quick nod, followed by another wary look at his sister, before he nodded again and grinned.

Gabe said nothing until Paul had disappeared inside the shop. Then he sat down at the small table and took a drink of lemonade.

Katherine did the same, hoping the liquid would make it easier to talk. When he still said nothing, she ventured a question. "What has upset you?"

His features, somewhat softened by Paul's presence, hardened, and he looked like a man on a death mission. "Cut the BS, Katie."

"No one calls me Katie these days. Please call me Katherine." She didn't need to be reminded of her youth, when everything had seemed possible.

"Katherine?"

She sighed. "Gabe, tell me why you're angry. And what it has to do with me."

"I don't know how you convinced her to do it, *Katie,* but I won't stand for it. You won't win." His hands clenched into fists.

It had to be Gran—Mrs. Dawson. She was the only connection between Katherine and Gabe. "What did your grandmother do?" she asked softly.

"You know exactly what she did. She wouldn't have done such an awful thing if you hadn't put her up to it."

"I visited your grandmother, Gabe, because—because she was lonely sometimes. But we never discussed you." Never, except for once. And Mrs. Dawson had promised never to reveal what Katherine had told her.

"Yeah, don't try that sob story on me. I talked to Gran every week."

"I know you did. She was very proud of your accomplishments." While they'd never discussed Gabe, Mrs. Dawson had always bragged on her grandson. Katherine had figured that was her due.

"So proud she didn't want to leave me anything?"

Katherine stared at him. When they'd dated, she'd known the Dawsons came from the wealthy side of town. His parents had had a nice house. His father had worked in Lubbock.

It wasn't until after Gabe left that her world had fallen apart, that she'd discovered his grandmother had money, too. While the Dawsons weren't as rich as some of the oil-rich families in town, Gabe's grandmother was well provided for.

"Did she leave it to your father?"

"Don't play games with me."

"Gabe, what are you talking about? I swear I don't know." And she was getting tired of being accused of something she didn't understand. "Now, you either explain what has upset you, or go away and stop bothering me."

"So you didn't know that she left me her estate on the condition that I marry you?"

His skepticism told her he didn't believe it. But

she was too stunned by what he'd said. Finally she muttered, "That can't be true."

"Oh, yeah, it's true. And you know what's even better? If I don't comply with her terms, you get half her estate and the other half goes to charity." He stood up, putting his fists on the table and leaning toward her. "But don't think you've won. I'm a pretty good lawyer. I'll find a way around it!"

Then he stalked back across the town square.

Katherine buried her face in her hands. Dear God, what had Gran done? Why? She knew Katie's secret. But that was no reason to—was that why? Because she'd broken down one day and let her think... She'd talk to Mac. If she refused the bequest, surely that would solve the problem.

Because Gabe was right.

Mrs. Dawson's solution wasn't going to happen.

GABE RETURNED to Mac's office because he didn't know where else to go. Would he be allowed to go to his grandmother's house without fulfilling the terms of the will? Should he see if the bed-and-breakfast on the square could take him? What was he going to do?

By the time he reached the reception room, he'd run out of steam. Fortunately, the secretary wasn't in sight, and he sank down in one of the leather chairs that filled the room.

Lordy, Katie looked good.

As good as she'd looked when she was eighteen and had broken his heart. Maybe even better. She had a woman's body and face, but she was still slender, with curves in all the right places.

The surge of desire that his anger had hidden hit him full blast. Damn it, he didn't want her!

Like hell he didn't.

He had to pull himself together, figure out what to do. He damned sure wasn't going to let Katie Peters have his grandmother's money. No way.

"You okay, pal?" Mac asked.

Gabe looked up to find his friend leaning against the door that opened onto the hall, sympathy on his face.

"Yeah, sure, I'm fine. It's been a shock, of course, but I'm fine." He was used to role-playing, hiding his weaknesses. A successful lawyer had to.

"Good. I called the other guys, and we wondered if you'd like to have dinner together. Cal married Jessica. You remember Jessica Hoya, don't you?" At Gabe's nod, Mac continued, "She's got a great restaurant, The Last Roundup. We can have steaks and catch up on everything."

"Yeah, fine, great idea. I'd like to see all of you before I leave town."

"Leave? You're not going to do what your grandmother asked?" Mac drew a couple of steps closer, concern on his face.

"Hey, I'm a lawyer. There'll be a way around it. I'm going to find a way."

Mac crossed over and sat down in the chair next to Gabe. "Buddy, I'm sorry, but she insisted I fix it so it couldn't be broken."

"Come on, Mac, you can't be serious. She can't force me into a marriage I don't want."

Mac sighed. "She left you an out—if Katherine marries someone else. But if you refuse and Katherine remains single, you lose everything."

"My marrying Katherine, as she calls herself now, isn't an option. So just cross that off your list. It's not going to happen."

"Then what are you going to do?"

"I don't know. Can I stay at Gran's place?"

"Sure. You've got a year. You don't lose anything for a year." He stood up and headed for his office. "I'll get the keys for you. I've had someone go in once a week and open up, dust a little. So everything should be in good shape."

Gabe sat there, waiting. When Mac came back into sight, he said, "I have another request."

"What's that?"

"I want to visit with your mothers."

"Mothers? Why? I mean, they'll be glad to see you, of course, but..."

"I need some lessons on matchmaking. Mrs. Katherine Hill is going to marry before the year is out...one way or another."

Chapter Two

"Alex, this is Katherine Hill at The Lemon Drop Shop."

"Hi, Katherine. How's everything going?"

Katherine didn't bother to pretend. "Not well. I have a problem. Do you have time to see me this afternoon?"

There was a pause and Katherine held her breath.

"Yes, I can talk to you at four-thirty. Does that work with your schedule?"

"Yes, thank you." The school rush would be slowing down by four-thirty, and her two employees could handle the business. She didn't think her talk with Alex would take too long. She'd asked for Mac, but he was booked for the rest of the afternoon, and Katherine couldn't wait that long to get legal advice.

AT FOUR-THIRTY, she crossed the square and entered the law office of Gibbons & Langford. She'd removed her apron, of course, but she wished she'd dressed up. Only, this morning, when she'd started her day at six, she hadn't expected to need legal advice.

Alex rose and came around the desk to greet her. "I haven't seen you in a while, Katherine. I had to give up those cinnamon rolls in the mornings. My doctor told me to cut back on sugar." She gestured to one of the chairs in front of her desk as she sat back down.

Katherine sat as she said, "Oh, I'm sorry. Is everything all right?"

"Yes, but I'm expecting again." Alex beamed.

"How wonderful! Your little girl is almost a year old, isn't she?"

"Yes. She'll be eighteen months when this one is born. But enough about me. Why don't you tell me why you're here."

"Do you have to inherit something if it's left to you?"

Alex frowned slightly. "Do you mean someone has left you something you don't want?"

"Yes, that's it, exactly." Katherine leaned back with a sigh, glad Alex grasped the situation.

"Do you want to give me details?"

"I guess so. Did you meet Mrs. Dawson?" Katherine thought everyone in town knew Mrs. Dawson, but Alex had only been there a couple of years.

"Yes, several times. Mac drew up her will just a few months ago and—she's the one who left you something?"

"I've been told that she did if…if certain conditions weren't met by the beneficiary." It was easier to think of Gabe as an impersonal term.

"What conditions?"

"Is it okay if I tell you? I mean, aren't wills supposed to be secret?"

"Who told you?"

Katherine licked her lips as she remembered Gabe's arrival in her shop, his anger, his—sexiness. "The beneficiary."

"Did he swear you to secrecy?" Alex asked.

"No. No, in fact, he shouted—that is, he intended to talk in front of everyone, but I got him to sit at a table outside and explain what was wrong."

"And was this person Gabe Dawson? Because I just met him a little while ago."

Katherine nodded.

"A handsome man," Alex observed, watching Katherine.

Katherine hated her fair complexion. It gave her away every time she was embarrassed. She looked at her clasped hands and muttered, "An angry man."

"But I understood he was the beneficiary. Why would he be angry?"

"Gran—Mrs. Dawson left him her estate on several conditions. The worst one is that he has to marry me."

Alex had been leaning back in her chair. She sat up abruptly, staring at Katherine. "You're kidding."

"No, I'm not. He said I must have persuaded her to write her will that way. But I didn't, I swear, Alex. We never discussed anything like that. I took her some cookies occasionally, and I would rent movies for her. We visited because sometimes she got lonely. But that's all, I promise."

"I believe you, Katherine," Alex said soothingly. She scratched her forehead. "So you want to know if you can reject the estate if you and Gabe don't marry?"

"There's no if. Gabe hasn't spoken to me in ten years, Alex. The only reason he approached me now was to chew me out."

"I'd like to see the will, but if Mac wrote it—" Her gaze flew to the closed door. "Wait a minute. I think I hear him." She slid around her desk and went to the door. Opening it, she called, "Mac?"

"Yeah, Alex, I'm back."

"Can you spare a minute?"

"Sure."

Alex moved back to her desk, and Mac came through the door, a smile on his face.

Until he saw Katherine.

"Uh-oh."

Even Alex seemed surprised by his reaction. "You know why Katherine is here?"

Mac sat on the edge of Alex's desk, facing Katherine. "I assume it has something to do with Mrs. Dawson's will. Right?"

Katherine nodded. "I don't want to take—how can I get my name out of it?"

"You can't."

His simple answer, without any legal mumbo jumbo, was what made Mac Gibbons such a popular lawyer. People wanted to hear the bottom line, without all the reasons.

"But there must be some way. He won't—a marriage between us is preposterous. He shouldn't have to give up his grandmother's estate because— surely, she didn't intend to harm Gabe." Katherine couldn't imagine the sweet woman she'd known doing anything to negatively affect her beloved Gabe.

"No, I don't think she did." Mac shot a look at Alex and rubbed the back of his neck before he said anything else. "Look, Katie, when our mothers did their matchmaking, a lot of ladies in town got the idea to follow in their footsteps. I tried to warn Mrs. Dawson that her idea would backfire on her, and Gabe. But she wouldn't listen."

"That's what the will says, that she has to marry Gabe? Or what happens?" Alex asked.

"If they don't marry, half the estate goes to Katie and the other half goes to charity. Unless Katie marries someone else before the year is up. You seeing anyone?" he suddenly asked, slewing around to face Katherine again.

"No! I'm not."

"I heard Jack Ledbetter was hanging around your house a lot," Mac said, a speculative look on his face.

Alex frowned. "But Jack's over fifty, maybe older. He's too old for you, Katherine."

"He's fifty-six," she said calmly. "And he is hanging around our house. But it's not me he's interested in."

Mac frowned. "Then who—your mother?" He grinned. "If you need any advice about this situation, let me know. Aunt Florence and Doc got married a year ago, you know."

Katherine grinned. "Thanks, but they're managing just fine without any assistance on my part." In fact, her mother's romance was one of the best things going in her life right now.

Alex brought them back to the topic at hand. "So, if you're not seeing anyone, and you won't marry Gabe—"

"As if he'd ask," Katherine muttered, interrupting.

Alex looked at Mac for confirmation. "Then there's nothing to be done?"

"I'm afraid that's true, Katie," Mac concurred. "Gabe said something about trying to prove his grandmother was incompetent when she made these arrangements, but I don't think he can."

"But if half of the estate comes to me, can I give it back to Gabe? Just return it?"

"Not without paying some taxes."

"But I can't afford that!" She was doing well with her shop, but there were a lot of demands on her income.

"What size estate are we talking about?" Alex asked quietly.

"She and her husband owned about a hundred and fifty acres and several wells were drilled on her property. The total, with land value and everything else, is around ten million," Mac said calmly.

Katherine almost fell out of her chair. "Good

heavens! Taxes on half of that would bankrupt me for life.''

Mac nodded, though he added, ''If you inherited it, of course, you could pay the taxes out of what you inherited.''

''I can't,'' Katherine said firmly. The money didn't matter. Taking his heritage from Gabe was the issue. And she couldn't do that.

Shaking his head, Mac said, ''Well, I'm not sure how this is going to work out. You sure you don't want to marry him?''

The way he asked his question made Katherine's heart ache. And made an answer impossible. What she wanted didn't matter. She'd rejected his marriage proposal when she was eighteen. He wouldn't ask again.

Standing, she offered her hand to Alex first and then Mac. ''Thanks for your help. Will you send me a bill? Or shall I leave you a check?''

Alex smiled. ''I'll send you a bill. If there's anything else I can do, let me know.''

''I will, thanks.'' Then she left their offices, still with no answers. And a lot of fears.

''What are you doing here?'' Gabe growled, moving in front of her as she stepped outside.

She jumped, surprised by his sudden appearance.

''Well?'' he demanded, his hands on his hips, glaring at her.

She had no intention of explaining what she'd been doing, and she knew Mac and Alex would be discreet. ''Excuse me,'' she murmured, and tried to step around him.

He reached out and grabbed her arm.

She thought she'd forgotten how her body responded to his touch. She thought the shivers that had coursed through her body the first time he'd touched his lips to hers, many years ago, couldn't possibly reoccur. She thought that part of her life was over.

Someone forgot to tell her body.

Jerking away, she retreated, her back coming up against the door she'd just closed. She lifted her chin and glared at him. "I have to go."

"You got someone waiting for you? Someone you're planning on marrying? Maybe you've promised some man a cushy life if he hangs around until the year is over."

She knew of only one way to escape him. And she was angry and scared enough to lie. "Yes, I have a man. What's it to you?"

"So marry him! That would solve my problem."

With sarcasm dripping from her words, she said, "Of course, solving your problem would be my first concern."

"It should be, since you caused it."

As he spoke, the door behind Katherine opened and Mac reached out to steady her as she almost lost her balance.

"Hi, there, Gabe. You're early."

Neither of them spoke, and Mac moved to Katherine's side and looked at them. "Everything okay?"

"Sure, everything's fine. I was trying to convince

Mrs. Hill to marry her latest man and solve my problem.''

Mac frowned and looked at Katherine.

She didn't bother explaining the contradiction of what she'd told him in Alex's office. With a smile, she excused herself, knowing Gabe wouldn't try to stop her with Mac there.

"Thanks again, Mac," she said hurriedly, and headed back to her shop.

Gabe turned to watch her walk away. He couldn't help it. A hunger raged through his body as his gaze followed her movement. What was wrong with him?

She'd so easily dismissed his love, his desire, ten years ago. And he'd vowed then never to get near her again. With good reason. He still couldn't trust his body. He wouldn't allow his heart to be put at risk again.

He spun around, anxious to dispel such thoughts. "What did she want?"

Mac shrugged his shoulders. "You know I can't tell you that. What a client says to her lawyer and her partner is privileged information."

"Well, maybe this man she's got will marry her before the end of the year." He should be glad about that idea. But the words he'd spoken troubled him. "Who is he?"

"Come on," Mac said, putting a hand on Gabe's shoulder and turning him toward The Last Roundup. "Let's go get a beer while we talk."

Gabe didn't fight Mac's suggestion. But he

wasn't going to let his question drop. "Well? Who's she dating?"

Mac kept walking.

"I'm not asking for privileged information, Mac. I know how it is in a small town. Everyone knows what's going on."

They reached the restaurant.

The hostess seated them in the back, at Cal and Jessica's special table, and Mac asked her to have the waitress bring two beers.

"It's not that it's privileged information, exactly, but we did discuss her, er, her personal life, and I feel a little uncomfortable—"

"Hey, Gabe, how are you?" Cal asked, interrupting Mac.

Gabe stood and shook hands with Cal Baxter, the sheriff in Cactus.

"Good to see you, Cal. I hear you've joined the married ranks with the other guys."

"Yeah. You should give it a try. We've all found it amazingly wonderful."

Gabe shook his head and sat down again.

The waitress arrived with two beers and Cal sent her off again to bring three more. "No sense in waiting until Spence and Tuck get here. We know they'll want one, too."

Gabe smiled and nodded.

"Now, what did I interrupt? What were you saying, Mac?"

Mac shrugged his shoulders again, not looking at either friend.

"He was being a lawyer," Gabe complained. "I

asked him a question, and he didn't want to answer it, afraid he'd be violating lawyer-client confidentiality.''

Cal cocked one eyebrow. ''You're a lawyer, Gabe. I guess you understand that.''

''Yeah, I understand. But I asked something that's common knowledge. I remember how it is here, even if I haven't lived here in ten years. Everyone knows everyone else's business.''

''True,'' Cal began, but he didn't continue because Tuck and Spence arrived. There were several minutes of greeting each other and exchanging comments about their lives. Then the beers arrived and the newcomers stopped talking to take a drink.

Cal leaned forward. ''Ask me your question. I'm not a lawyer.''

''Cal—'' Mac began, but Gabe ignored his friend.

''I want to know who's the man in Katherine's life.''

Cal sat back in his chair and stared at Gabe.

''Which Katherine?'' Spence asked, frowning.

Tuck stuck his elbow in Spence's ribs. ''Don't you remember? Gabe and Katie were—friends,'' he hurriedly said after receiving a glare from Gabe.

Cal took his time. He leaned forward and clasped his hands on the table. With a sideways look at Mac, he said, ''The only man I've heard about is Jack Ledbetter.''

''Who's that?'' Gabe demanded, a sick feeling filling his stomach at hearing a name, forcing him to realize the man was real.

Spence stared. "You're kidding. He's too old for Katie."

Those words got Gabe's attention. "Too old? How old is he? Who is he?"

"You remember Jack Ledbetter," Tuck insisted. "He and his wife lived about ten miles out of town. She raised German shepherds. Didn't your dad buy you one?"

"That's right," Gabe said with a frown, recalling old memories. The dog, Jericho, died while he was away at college. "Are they divorced?"

"No. His wife died of cancer a couple of years ago," Cal explained, but he didn't answer Gabe's other question.

"Spence is right. He's our fathers' age. What is she doing dating someone that old? What's the matter with her? Is she looking for someone to—" He broke off abruptly, unwilling to say that he suspected Katie was looking for a meal ticket.

"Yeah, I heard about Jack," Tuck said, "but I heard it was her mother he was interested in."

Gabe didn't want to admit the hope that leaped in his throat at those words. "Her mother?"

"Yeah, you remember her father died her senior year in high school," Tuck said. "Katie's mother pretty much fell apart. Katie's the one who pulled the family together. She's worked like a dog ever since then to take care of all of them."

Other comments were made, but Gabe didn't hear them. He'd forgotten about Katie's father's death. He'd tried to comfort her, of course, and she'd assured him everything was fine. He'd been coming home on weekends to see her, but he was finishing his senior year at Texas Tech and had a lot going on.

"What do you mean, she took care of all of them?" Gabe asked abruptly, interrupting Spence, who had made a flattering comment about Katie's shop.

Tuck raised one eyebrow. "Don't you remember?"

"We moved to Dallas that summer so I could start law school in the fall." After he'd proposed to Katie and been rejected, he'd wanted out of town. His parents had decided to move to Dallas, too. His mother had never been happy in the small town.

"And you didn't keep in touch?" Spence asked, a puzzled frown on his face.

"No." Nothing more. He wasn't going to remind his friends that the woman he'd loved had stomped all over him and walked away.

Tuck explained, "Katie took a day job at the grocery store and worked nights as a waitress."

"Was she saving for college?" She'd talked about going to Tech.

"No," Cal said. "She was paying the bills. Her dad never was much of a provider, but with him gone, they had a lot of bills. With five more kids and a mother who didn't know how to earn money, Katie became the breadwinner for everyone."

A sick feeling was building in Gabe's stomach. "But she married. I mean, her husband must've helped out, brought in money."

Mac snorted in derision. "Yeah, right. Darrell Hill came to town after you left. He worked at the gas station. After they married, he started showing up for work less and less, until he got fired."

"Doesn't seem like he was much help," Gabe muttered. The protective feelings that surged through him were ridiculous. She hadn't wanted him, or his help. He'd promised to help her get her college degree, too. But she'd said no.

No one said anything.

"How did he die?" Gabe finally asked.

Without any expression, Cal said, "He hit a tree going eighty miles an hour."

"Drunk?" Gabe asked, determined to know the worst.

"Oh, yeah. We're lucky he didn't take anyone with him." Cal shook his head. "Drinking and driving is about the stupidest thing I know."

They all nodded in solemn agreement. Then Tuck asked a question about Gabe's life in Dallas and the conversation lightened.

Gabe, however, couldn't get the earlier tale out of his head. He still had questions. But only Katie could answer them. And if he asked, if he dug into the past, she'd know that—she'd think that he was even more stupid than her dead husband.

She'd believe he still cared for a woman who'd rejected him ten long years ago.

Chapter Three

The Lemon Drop Shop closed its doors at six o'clock.

For the first time since she'd opened her shop, Katherine was counting the minutes.

"Are my pies ready?" Mabel Baxter asked.

"Yes, they are, Mrs. Baxter. Let me get them," Katherine replied with a smile. Mabel Baxter had been one of her early supporters and, as a town social lion, where she had gone, others had followed. Katherine owed her a lot.

She brought the two boxed pies from the storeroom and handed them over the counter.

As Mabel counted out the payment, she said, "I heard Gabe Dawson is back in town."

"Yes, I believe he is," Katherine said, hoping no one noticed the tremor in her voice.

"His grandmother was so proud of him. She wanted him to return to Cactus to settle down."

Katherine took the money and thanked Mabel, praying the conversation would end.

"You were high school sweethearts, weren't you?" Mabel continued.

"We dated my senior year, but Gabe was a senior at Tech. Too many years between us." A simple explanation. That was the best.

"I guess so. I wonder if he's married. Well, see you later," Mabel said, giving her a cheerful smile after delivering the dreadful thought.

Of course he wasn't married. If he had been, then Gran wouldn't have written that horrible will. Katherine breathed deeply, calming her rocketing nerves. Until another thought hit her.

That didn't mean he didn't have a "significant other." Maybe that explained his anger. He loved someone and hadn't told Gran about it.

Poor Gabe.

Ten years ago, when she'd refused his marriage proposal, she'd been proud of her selflessness. Until he left town and the pain set in. But she'd had little choice. She couldn't have walked away from her mother and brothers and sisters.

"I've cleaned the kitchen," Evelyn reported, disrupting Katherine's thoughts.

"Thanks, Evelyn. Do we need any supplies?"

"Just eggs. Mr. Stottlemyer brought a delivery of carrots, sugar and flour this afternoon while you were out."

"Great. I'll see you tomorrow then," Katherine said, checking her watch. Six o'clock had finally arrived. She walked around the counter and flipped the sign on the door to indicate the bakery was closed, then locked it.

"Mary didn't sound like she felt good when she left," Evelyn added with a frown. "If she can't come in the morning, you call me, okay?"

"Thanks, Evelyn, I will."

She wouldn't have any choice. She arrived at six each morning to start the baking for the day. The Last Roundup bought four carrot cakes each morning, freshly baked. Since this restaurant had been franchised in Lubbock, she was in negotiations to provide cakes for all of their locations. Then there were the other baked goods, including cinnamon rolls, for the early arrivals.

After mopping the restaurant area, Katherine turned out the lights and headed for her truck. Actually, it was an old Chevy Blazer. In the back, Katherine's two brothers had removed the second seat and replaced it with racks so she could deliver large orders. Lately, she'd even baked some wedding cakes.

She pulled up beside the house she'd lived in since she was a little girl. It wasn't an elegant home, but it had housed her and her family for a quarter of a century. They'd even managed to paint it a couple of years ago, the entire family pitching in.

Katherine smiled. She had a wonderful family. All the kids worked hard, never complained. Except for Susan, she thought with a sigh.

Her youngest sister appeared at her car door, as if she'd conjured her up with that thought. "Are you going to get out, or sit there all night?"

Katherine smiled and opened her car door. "I was just resting a minute. How was school today?"

Susan rolled her eyes and started walking toward the house.

Obviously the wrong question.

Her mother had dinner on the table. Katherine gave a grateful sniff, before she crossed the kitchen to kiss her mother's cheek. "Everything smells delicious, Mom."

"That's because *Jack's* joining us," Susan snapped, glaring at her mother.

"I—I didn't think you'd mind," Margaret Peters said, her anxious gaze on Katherine.

Katherine ignored her sister's reaction and hugged her mother. "Of course I don't mind. We need to thank him for the work he did on the chicken coop, anyway. I think the chickens have been laying more eggs now that the roof doesn't leak."

Susan gave a sound of disgust and left the kitchen.

"Katie, I don't think—"

Margaret's timorous tones ate away at Katherine's stomach. "Don't worry, Mom. Suse will get over it."

She hoped her sister would mature enough to stop interfering in her mother's chance at happiness. Margaret had wilted when her beloved husband had died. She'd had no idea how to go on. In the passing years, she'd grown stronger, helping Katherine with her business, taking care of the younger children. Katherine had encouraged her to make decisions, a new experience for Margaret.

Just a few months ago, Jack Ledbetter had asked

about leasing some of their acreage. Because of Katherine's hours, he'd come over after dinner one evening.

Katherine recognized the attraction that sparked between the two older people. With Margaret's shyness, the interest needed some careful nurturing. But Katherine had enthusiastically supported Jack's efforts.

Susan was the only one objecting.

The sound of a car engine signaled Jack's arrival and Margaret's cheeks turned bright red. "I—I think Jack's here."

"Yeah. I'll call the kids." Only Paul and Susan remained at home.

Once they were all seated around the table, passing bowls of delicious food, the subject Katherine had hoped to avoid came up.

"I hear Gabe Dawson is back in town. Didn't think he'd come back after burying his grandmother," Jack said, smiling at Margaret.

The sudden silence made Jack stare at the others.

"What did I say?" he asked, frowning.

"Nothing at all, Jack," Katherine assured him, but she kept her gaze fixed on her dinner plate.

"He came to the shop," Paul muttered.

"What did he say? Is he moving back to town?" Susan asked, excitement in her voice for the first time. Like Paul, she'd adored Gabe.

"No!" Katherine snapped, and then moderated her voice. "He's just here to settle Mrs. Dawson's estate. I'm sure he'll only be here a day or two."

"You talked to him?" Margaret asked.

"Um, yes, I did." Katherine didn't add any details. She certainly wasn't going to reveal Gran's ridiculous will.

She knew her mother wouldn't pry, and fortunately Jack asked a question about Paul's school activities that distracted him. But she could feel Susan's stare, even though she never looked at her baby sister.

When the meal ended, she sent Jack and Margaret into the living room. Then she turned to Susan. "Which job do you want? Gathering the eggs or cleaning the dishes?"

"Neither one," Susan protested, her bottom lip protruding.

"I'll get the eggs, Katie," Paul hurriedly said. "I have to milk Betsy anyway."

"And that's why Susan will gather the eggs," Katherine said firmly. "We all have to do our share."

"Raine and Diane aren't doing anything, and you send them money all the time."

Katherine pressed her lips together. Then she relaxed them into a smile. "And hopefully I'll be able to do the same for you. They worked hard while they were growing up. And they both work now, after class every day."

Susan opened her mouth to protest, but Katherine had had a long day. She wasn't willing to argue with her sister tonight. "Go get the eggs," she ordered in a no-nonsense voice and began gathering the dishes.

Susan stood there, and Katherine feared she'd

have to have a showdown with her little sister. Finally Susan stomped from the house, her displeasure evident.

"I don't know what's wrong with her," Paul said, worry in his voice.

"It's okay, Paul. Everyone can't be perfect like you," Katherine told him, smiling.

"Aw, sis!" he protested, and hurried after Susan.

Katherine sank down into the nearest chair and buried her face in her hands. Finding solitude was the most difficult feat in her life.

She wanted to examine the feelings that had filled her when Gabe had suddenly reappeared in her life. She wanted to indulge in memories that made her weak with longing.

Maybe it was best that she couldn't.

Too many chores awaited her.

GABE SAT IN HIS GRANDMOTHER'S rocking chair on the back porch of her home, listening to the silence. Sometimes, in the city, it seemed he never found the silence that the countryside provided.

Or all the glittering stars.

No lights to compete with their brightness. He hadn't turned on a light. He hadn't even opened the door to Gran's house. As if he were afraid to go in.

Ridiculous. He'd gone into her house when he'd come for her funeral. But he hadn't been alone. His parents had accompanied him. In spite of the fact that his mother and Gran hadn't gotten along, even his mother had mourned the old lady's passing.

And they'd all felt guilty.

Gran had been left in Cactus alone. He'd been reluctant to come visit because of Katie. Oh, he'd come occasionally, but not as often, or for as long, as he should have. Gran always said she understood.

She'd come to Dallas occasionally. He'd bought her a plane ticket every time he could convince her to leave Cactus. The last couple of years, that hadn't been often.

Katie had visited her.

That information had slipped out in her protestations of innocence. Which only made her seem more guilty. She'd brought Gran cookies and videos to watch.

He should have known. Even if she did have evil intentions, Katie wouldn't forget Gran. When the two of them had been dating, they'd spent a lot of time at Gran's house. His mother hadn't seemed too welcoming to Katie. She'd wanted her son to date someone at Texas Tech. His own kind, she'd said.

Even though she'd never been rude to Katie, as far as he knew, Katie had sensed his mother's disapproval. Katie had been reluctant to go to his home. Her home had been a three-ring circus, with her five younger brothers and sisters and her parents present. So they'd come to Gran's.

Every room in the house held memories.

Some he'd like to forget.

Which explained why he was still sitting on the porch. Not that he'd been here that long. Dinner with his friends had dragged out, as they'd talked about old times.

They were good friends. He'd made other friends in Dallas, while attending law school, but the friendships weren't as deep, as satisfying, as those he'd made as a child.

But even with them, his best friends, he couldn't discuss his difficulties.

He stood up, ignoring the creak of the rocker, and strode to the back door. It was locked, which took him by surprise. Gran had never locked her doors, but Mac had had the place locked up, of course. He dug out the keys Mac had given him and unlocked the door.

The house smelled fresh, witnessing Mac's remark that he'd had someone come in on a regular basis. Gabe reached out and clicked on the overhead light.

The big kitchen was neat and tidy. Too neat. It looked barren, compared to the clutter Gran had always had. Gabe tossed the keys on top of the pine table and went back out to his Mercedes. He'd picked up a few necessities at the grocery.

Waking up in the morning with no coffee in the house wasn't something he was interested in doing. He could go without food for a while, but not without coffee.

He pulled out Gran's percolator, a fancy one with a timing device. He'd given it to her last Christmas. Sighing, he realized she'd never used it. The tags were still on it.

Preparing the pot and setting the timer for eight in the morning, figuring he'd sleep in after his long day, he considered going to bed.

But he didn't think he could go to sleep until he made a plan of action. He'd carried in his suitcase and briefcase along with the groceries. He put his briefcase on the table and pulled out a chair.

With a clean legal pad and pen, he felt more confident that he could find a way out of this mess. The tools of his trade. He began listing the problems. Then he looked for solutions.

Finally he accepted what Mac had told him. The will was unbreakable. He had one option, other than the impossible one of marrying Katie. He had to get her married to someone else. That shouldn't be too hard, he decided, anger surging up in him again. She'd already married once.

He remembered the care he'd taken with the inexperienced Katie. His father had warned him about unprotected sex. He'd taken that warning to heart, always carrying condoms. But Katie had never been intimate with anyone. He'd wanted her first time to be special. With him.

His grandmother had taken a cruise with some of the other ladies from Cactus. She'd asked Gabe to stay at her place over the weekend. He'd brought Katie there and made love to her, in his bed.

He'd protected her, loved her. Adored her.

The next weekend, he'd intended to propose to her. But her father died in the middle of the week. He'd come back for the funeral. Katie had scarcely had time for him, except to fall into his arms for one brief hug.

Now, looking back, he realized how selfish he'd been. Shame filled him at his egocentric response to Katie's earth-shattering experience. All he'd been able to think of were his plans for the future. For the two of them.

But she hadn't made any effort to explain. To ask him to wait. In fact, when he'd returned a couple of weeks later after his college graduation to finally bare his heart to her, she'd told him she'd met someone else.

The pain had been so intense, so shattering, he'd been unable to even ask questions. To wonder at the sudden turn in their relationship.

Unable to face those memories, Gabe ripped the top sheet from the legal pad. Immediately he began a list of all the single men he knew in Cactus. There weren't all that many, he realized. Most of the young people had left. These days they were attracting more industry to Cactus.

The guys were telling him about a billionaire who had settled in Cactus and was building a factory outside town. But the young people who were staying were years younger than Katie. She was twenty-eight now.

He'd have to ask the matchmakers. Mabel Baxter and her cronies. They'd know who was available.

He headed a column Things To Do.

1. Visit with the matchmakers.

2. Talk to Jack Ledbetter.

Reluctantly he added a third.

3. Make a decision about my job.

He'd taken a week's vacation to settle Gran's estate, but it appeared it was going to take a lot longer. Once he took possession of the house, as he had tonight, he had to remain living there for a year.

He could hardly commute to Dallas.

Tucking the legal pad and pen back into his brief-case, he shut it and stood. It was too late to make any decisions tonight. Tomorrow, he'd get a fresh start.

He picked up his suitcase and headed down the hall to the bedroom that had always been his. The bedroom where he'd first made love to Katie.

No. He'd use the guest room. It held no memories for him. Neither of Gran nor Katie. It had always been kept in pristine condition, in case a visitor had dropped in. Gran was a proud housekeeper. Toward the end, he'd hired a neighbor to come in twice a week and clean for her. She'd hated that.

He opened the door to the guest room, finding it ready for a last-minute guest, as he'd known it would be. The decor was a little too feminine for his taste, but he'd suffer the flowered comforter and drapes tonight. After all, if he wasn't staying, it wouldn't matter. And if he was—

Nope. He couldn't think about that tonight. He wanted to sleep, to forget the past, to deny the future. He was back in Cactus. That was enough for now.

OLD HABITS WERE HARD to break.

Gabe was awake at seven. In Dallas, he normally hit the shower at six-thirty, so he supposed he'd actually, technically, broken his early-morning habit, but there was no reason to roll out of bed this morning.

And, damn it, the coffee wouldn't be ready until eight.

With a groan, he padded into the kitchen and adjusted the timer until he heard it turn on. Then he headed for the shower. By the time he finished, the coffee would be ready.

He was leaning against the counter, downing his first cup of coffee, when he heard a car in the driveway. A smile settled in place when he saw the sheriff's official car. Cal had come to see him.

Then it occurred to him that maybe there was a problem. The phone wasn't connected, but he had a cell phone. His parents would have called if—

He hurried to the back door. "Come in, Cal. Is anything wrong?"

"Not a thing. Thought you might like a little breakfast," he said, holding up a white paper bag.

A cinnamon aroma filled the air and caused Gabe's stomach to growl. "How'd you guess?" he asked with a grin.

"Not hard to do. Any more coffee?"

"You bet. Have a seat while I pour you a cup."

Soon the two men were seated, munching on sausage rolls, with two fat cinnamon rolls waiting.

"These are great," Gabe said. "You must be the luckiest man in the world."

"How's that?" Cal asked, his eyes closed as he savored another bite.

"To have a wife like Jessica."

Cal grinned. "You won't hear me complaining.

Wait until you meet my son. Then you'll really know how lucky I am.''

''How old is he?''

''Almost a year old. He's starting to learn to walk. Which is a good thing, because Tuck's been bragging about his little girl for a month now. Did you know that girls learn to walk before boys? Can you believe that?''

The disgust in Cal's voice tickled Gabe. He chuckled and it felt good. He hadn't been that happy when he'd awakened, but a good friend could cheer up a guy.

''I think that's so girls can get a head start running away from boys.''

''Yeah,'' Cal replied, his face suddenly serious. ''I've sure had some cases where I've wished the woman would run. Domestic violence is ugly.''

An alarming thought filled Gabe. ''Katie never— I mean, her husband didn't—''

''Not that I know of. But he didn't appreciate her. That's for sure.''

''Maybe she was a lousy wife,'' Gabe muttered, picking up the cinnamon roll and sniffing it.

''I doubt it. Even if she was, she'd make up for a lot of sins, being able to make these.''

Gabe had just taken a big bite. He almost choked on it before he could speak. ''You mean Katie made these?''

''Well, of course. I stopped by The Lemon Drop Shop on my way over here.''

Chapter Four

Gabe swallowed the bite of cinnamon roll and cleared his throat. "I, uh, assumed Jessica made these."

"Nope. She was sleeping in this morning since Rick has a cold. He wakes up a lot at night. She didn't get much sleep."

Gabe frowned. "What does Doc say?"

"It's a cold," Cal said with a shrug. "I've adjusted to the problems with children. You should have seen me the first month after we brought him home. Jessica called me an alarmist."

Gabe's brows soared. "You? You're always the calm one."

"Not when it comes to my kid. You'll see when you have your own," Cal assured him.

Gabe sipped his coffee, unable to agree. He figured he'd never have children because he never intended to marry. His romantic experience hadn't led to much optimism in that area. But the look of bliss on Cal's face made him want to have children.

When he'd thought he and Katie would share a

future, he'd pictured their children, a little girl with Katie's long blond hair, a pink bow in it, a rough-and-tumble boy, playing with a dog like Jericho. Life had looked perfect until Katie's bomb exploded.

"Who did Katie date after me?"

His abrupt question got Cal's attention. He frowned. "You mean ten years ago? When you moved to Dallas?"

"Yeah. Ten years ago."

Cal stared at the opposite wall, thinking, and Gabe held his breath. He prayed it wasn't one of his friends. He'd hate to try to beat up Spence or Tuck or Mac.

"No one."

Gabe stared at Cal. "What do you mean, no one? There was someone. You must not remember."

Cal laughed. "Right. A beautiful lady like Katie, staying in town, staying at home on Saturday night, and you think we didn't notice? For a while, we figured you two had an understanding. That things had to be postponed because of her dad's death. Everyone kind of left her alone."

Frowning, Gabe thought back to what Katie had told him. "Maybe it was someone from out of town."

"Oh, yeah. We never notice strangers in Cactus."

"You're being sarcastic," Gabe protested.

"Why are you asking? Did you two have an understanding? I mean, it seemed kind of harsh to think you'd abandoned her when things got bad."

Gabe heard the note of censure in his friend's voice and it hurt. He said, "I didn't abandon her. I asked her to marry me, move to Dallas with me." Cal just stared at him, and he added, "I was focused on—on myself. I didn't realize how hard things were for her."

"We can all be selfish bastards at times. But that's better than walking away from her, leaving her hoping."

Gabe wasn't sure about that. He was beginning to feel guilty about his behavior ten years ago. And it made him mad. She could have said something!

"So, when you asked her to marry you, she said…" Cal waited for him to fill in the blank.

"She said she'd fallen for someone else." After a glimpse of the sympathy in Cal's gaze, Gabe looked away. "I guess she lied."

"Probably. It was a bad time for all of them. Maybe she couldn't think about leaving her family."

"I would have waited!" Gabe muttered. She hadn't even given him a chance.

"For ten years?"

"Hell! They could have moved with us. We would've worked something out."

Both men sat in silence, thinking about the events ten years ago. Finally Gabe acknowledged, "Okay, maybe that's not realistic, but—"

"Maybe you should be having this conversation with Katie. You might be able to work something out that would take care of that pesky will."

"No!" Gabe yelled, overreacting, he knew.

"No," he repeated more calmly. "Too much water under the bridge." He thought about the husband she'd had, the years, the…hurt. Nope, he wasn't willing to offer his heart again, to be carved up at will.

Cal shoved his chair back from the table. "So, what have you got planned for the day?"

"I've made a list of things I need to do. I suppose I'll see how many I can accomplish."

"Are you planning on staying?"

Gabe looked at Cal, a question in his gaze, as he said, "I'm thinking about it. If I have any chance of inheriting Gran's estate, I have to live here a year."

"We'd like having you around," Cal said warmly, answering Gabe's unasked question. "We sometimes rodeo on Saturdays. Think you can still ride?"

Gabe grinned. "Better than you, cowboy. If I'm going to stay, I might buy a couple of horses. Would Spence or Tuck have any to sell?"

"I reckon. They usually do. In fact, the last time I was over at Spence's, he had a fine-looking gelding. I was thinking about him myself, but I've already got more than I can ride."

"I'll check with him," Gabe said, reaching for his briefcase and his list.

"You and your lists," Cal teased, rising to his feet.

"Hey, it's the only way to stay organized." Gabe stood and extended his hand. "Thanks for the breakfast…and the friendship, Cal."

"No thanks needed. I enjoyed the breakfast...and you already had the friendship."

THE THREE GENTLEMEN in suits were not dressed like the normal customers of The Lemon Drop Shop. In spite of the distraction Katherine felt, scanning the town square for any sign of Gabe, she went on red alert when the men entered the shop.

"Is Mrs. Hill here?" one of them asked as he stepped forward.

"I'm Katherine Hill. How may I help you?"

"We're from the TGM Corporation, owner of The Last Roundup franchises in Lubbock."

"Are you Mr. Frizzell?" When the man nodded, she added, "I believe I spoke to you on the phone."

"That's correct. We thought it would be a good idea to taste your product."

When she made the four carrot cakes for The Last Roundup each day, she also made one for her shop, which she sold by the slice. Since the gentlemen had arrived before lunch, she still had some available.

"Of course. If you'll be seated, I'll bring you each a sample."

Evelyn and Mary were working in the kitchen. Katherine stepped through the doors. "Can one of you watch the counter for a few minutes? I've got a business meeting."

Though their eyes were filled with questions, the two ladies didn't ask anything. Katherine figured they'd seen her tension. There would be a lot of profit in selling twelve to fifteen carrot cakes every morning. She charged twenty-five dollars a cake, which still left a large profit margin for the restaurants.

She prepared a tray with pieces of cake and cups of coffee and carried it through to the table the men had chosen. Just as she finished serving them and sat down to discuss their interest, the door was shoved open, the bell over it ringing mightily.

"Katie, I want to talk to you," Gabe Dawson announced, as if his needs had to be met at once.

"Excuse me," Katherine murmured to the men, and crossed over to Gabe's side. "I can't talk right now. I have a business meeting. I should be free in half an hour."

Gabe glowered at first her and then the men. "I won't take long," he insisted.

Katherine gritted her teeth. "Not now, Gabe." Then she turned around and hurried to the other table. She didn't know what Gabe would do, but she prayed he wouldn't mess things up.

"Gabe Dawson!" Mary called out. "It's good to see you, boy. Why don't you sit down and let me pour you a cup of coffee. And we've got a couple of sausage rolls left over from this morning. If you don't eat them, we'll just have to throw them out."

Katherine vowed to give Mary a bonus if she improved Gabe's mood, as well as kept him occupied until she could finish with the businessmen.

They had already begun eating their cake. Katherine could tell by the expressions on their faces and the quickly disappearing cake that half the battle was won.

Mr. Frizzell daintily wiped his mouth with the lemon-yellow paper napkin after scarfing down his piece. He cleared his throat. "Yes, um, well, very tasty cake, Mrs. Hill."

"Thank you."

"This was baked this morning?" the second man asked.

"Yes, it was. I bake four cakes every morning for The Last Roundup and simply make an extra for the shop."

"I guess you don't have much left over," the third man, a little more rotund than the other two, asked, beaming at her.

"No, I don't," she agreed with a smile.

"May we see your baking facilities?" Mr. Frizzell asked, and Katherine proudly led the way to her kitchen. She'd been in business for five years. Each year she'd plowed as much money as she could into updating her facilities. Now the large room was state-of-the-art, with four large professional ovens on one wall.

"Could you produce, say, three cakes each for our three locations in Lubbock each day, in addition to Jessica's order?" Mr. Frizzell asked.

"Yes, of course. But I can't deliver to Lubbock. I don't have the personnel for that." She held her breath. With Paul ready for college in the fall and Susan right behind him the next year, the extra profit would come in handy.

"No, we understand. We can take care of delivery, but the cakes would need to be picked up by nine-thirty each morning."

"That wouldn't be a problem."

"And, since we're ordering in quantity, I suppose you could give us a discount?"

Katherine paused, tempted to cut her profit to insure she got their business, but she knew how much profit Jessica made on her cakes. And she knew she made a good product. Taking a deep breath and praying they wouldn't walk out, she smiled and said, "I'm sorry, Mr. Frizzell. While I'd like your business, I use the best ingredients in my product and I can't lower my price."

All three men frowned.

"Very well. We'll let you know our decision," the head man said, and they shook hands with her and left.

Katherine remained in the kitchen, standing there with her face buried in her hands, sure she'd just made a huge mistake.

"Katie!" Gabe snapped from the kitchen door.

She lowered her hands and turned around. As usual, she had no time for privacy.

"Yes, Gabe?"

"Do you have time to work me into your schedule?" he drawled, implying she'd put him off just to be difficult.

With a sigh, she picked up the decorating tube Mary had abandoned to work the counter and finished decorating the cake her assistant had been working on. "If you can talk while I work."

She hadn't looked at him after that first brief glance. When he said nothing, she finally looked up.

He was staring at Evelyn, who was pouring batter into several cupcake pans.

Evelyn, seeming to feel his stare, looked up. "Oh! Oh, do you want me to go to the counter?" she asked, looking at Katherine.

"No," Katherine replied.

"Yes," Gabe ordered.

Katherine's gaze told Evelyn to go back to work. Then she said calmly, "The last I checked, this was my shop and Evelyn worked for me. Right?"

"I need to talk to you alone."

His husky voice sent shivers down her spine, but she stood her ground.

"Then come back after the school rush, around four thirty or five. Maybe I can spare you five minutes then."

"Damn it, Katie, this is—"

"I told you to call me Katherine."

"Fine, Katherine! I want information now. I can't waste my entire day waiting for you to deign to give me five minutes."

"Take it or leave it," she replied, stubbornly continuing with her work.

"Is Jack Ledbetter the one you said—is he the one?"

Katherine knew at once what he meant. And she didn't want any more questions in front of Evelyn, who was a dear soul but loved gossip more than anyone in Cactus. Taking a deep breath, she said, "Yes, he is."

His voice sounding like a growl, he muttered, "I

should have known.'' Then he stomped out of the kitchen.

Katherine sagged against the counter and closed her eyes. First she'd lost the cake order. Then she'd had to deal with an angry Gabe.

"What about Jack?" Evelyn asked.

"I think Gabe has heard that Jack is sweet on Mom. I guess he doesn't approve."

"Oh, I think it's wonderful. I'm happy for your mom," Evelyn enthused. "Why, I remember…"

Katherine nodded at the appropriate moments as Evelyn recounted ancient history, letting her mind drift to the handsome man who was driving her crazy.

KATIE'S CALM WORDS kept playing over and over in his mind. "Yes, he is."

She didn't even appear to be ashamed to be dating a man old enough to be her father. Maybe even her grandfather! Okay, so maybe that was an exaggeration. But you'd think she'd be embarrassed to be thought a gold digger.

He gripped the wheel more tightly, wishing he could squeeze some sense into Katie. If she was that desperate for money— He broke off that dangerous thought. After all, he hadn't offered to marry her.

She didn't need to marry *him* to get money.

She could inherit Gran's estate by not marrying anyone. Not even Jack Ledbetter.

"And that's why I'm going to up the ante," he muttered to himself. He turned the steering wheel so the car pulled off the main road onto Jack Ledbetter's gravel driveway, parked and got out.

The man stepped out of the barn, several dogs at his heels. The dogs distracted Gabe since they closely resembled his dog, Jericho. His stomach didn't feel good, either.

But he was going to take care of things…today.

"Well, I heard you were back in town, Gabe. Welcome. How are you?"

Hell, he didn't want the man to be friendly. He crossed the distance between them and took the hand Jack extended. The dogs sniffed at his boots.

"These two look a lot like Jericho," he muttered.

"They're his kinfolk. Well, at least she is. I got the boy from a man in Lubbock. Didn't want too much inbreeding," Jack said, smiling easily. "You looking for a dog? I've got four pups to sell."

That thought distracted Gabe. A dog? In Dallas, there'd been no point to having a dog. He was never home enough to spend any time with a pet. But a sudden yearning in his heart told him how much he'd missed having a dog.

"I might." He cleared his throat. "But I have something else to talk about first."

Jack's eyebrows, black mixed with gray, rose up. "Well, sure thing. Want to come in? I can put on a pot of coffee."

Gabe didn't want any more coffee. What he had to say wouldn't take long. If he could only figure out how to say it when the man was being so damn nice. "A glass of ice water would be better," he said.

"Yeah, you're right. The days are warming up, aren't they? Come on." Jack led the way to his back porch and into the kitchen.

Once they were seated at the table, glasses of ice water in front of them, Jack looked at him expectantly.

Gabe swallowed. "I heard you're thinking of marrying again."

It should have been amusing to see the older man's cheeks flush with embarrassment. But the whole thing was too painful for Gabe to laugh.

"Well, I haven't said anything, but I guess the townfolk can see how besotted I am," Jack said with a nod. "She's a sweet thing."

"She's a little young for you, isn't she?" Gabe snapped. Then he wanted to bang his head against the wall. He was supposed to be encouraging the man, not talking him out of marrying Katie.

Jack's eyebrows rose again. "Not that much. And I'm in real good health. I went to see Doc just last week to make sure. I don't want her marrying me if I'm going to be a problem for her."

"Right," Gabe agreed. "That was considerate of you. What did Doc say?"

Jack grinned. "Aw, he recommended it. You know he and Florence got married last year?"

"Florence Gibbons?" Gave asked, distracted. "Mac's aunt?"

"Yeah. We had a busy time, what with all those boys getting married, too. Thought they'd rename the town Cupid instead of Cactus," Jack said with a chuckle. "You married yet?"

"No. And not planning on it, either. Have you set a date yet?" Now he expected Jack to stall. He figured Katie would have made it clear that they couldn't marry for a year. Until she had her money safe. Then she'd have her meal ticket and a husband to support her, too.

He gritted his teeth.

"I'd like to make it as soon as possible. Katherine said—"

"I bet I know what she said," Gabe retorted. "But I think you should ignore her and go ahead."

"Ignore her?" Jack asked, an anxious look on his face. "You mean she's against it? But she said—"

"I'm sure she just wants to postpone it, Jack. She probably wants to go ahead with the wedding, but not until next year."

Jack blinked several times in surprise. "That wasn't the impression she gave me."

"When did you last talk to her about it?"

"I talked to her after my visit with Doc."

"Ah. Before I came back to town." That figures. She didn't know she had the chance to have money without marrying Jack. Not that there was anything wrong with the man. He wasn't even bad looking for fifty-six.

"What would that have to do with anything?" Jack asked, bewildered.

"Nothing, I'm sure. I was just thinking aloud." Or not thinking at all. Now what? "Well, I'd encourage you to strike while the iron is hot. Who knows what will happen next week."

Jack rapped the table with his fist. "You're right. I'm going to go propose tonight. There's no point waiting. I may be healthy, but I don't want to waste time."

"Great idea. I wish you well," Gabe said, standing. And definitely feeling sick to his stomach.

"Thanks, Gabe, for the good advice."

Now he really felt guilty.

"Say, did you want to see any of the pups for sale?" Jack asked.

"Sure. Do any of them look like Jericho?"

"I believe they all do," he assured Gabe with a grin. "My dogs breed true." He stood. "Come on out to the barn."

Five minutes later, Gabe was the proud owner of a German shepherd puppy.

"Your timing was perfect. I just decided yesterday they were ready to be sold." Jack reached over and stroked the head of the puppy. "She's a sweet one, she is. What are you going to name her?"

Gabe's mind flashed to Katie…again. He couldn't name the dog after her. Everyone would figure that out. And besides, he didn't need a constant reminder of her. "Cinnamon. I'm going to name her Cinnamon," he said suddenly. That was better than Lemon, or Sausage Roll or—

"Good choice. Her fur reminds me a little of those cinnamon rolls Katie bakes. You tasted those yet?"

"Yeah."

Jack beamed at him. "I reckon when I marry Margaret I'll get all I want of those for free. Some deal, isn't it? A sweet woman and a sweet break-fast.'' He laughed at his little joke.

Gabe stood, turned to stone. Margaret? He was going to marry Margaret? Katie's mom? Tuck had been right. And Katie had lied to him.

Slow anger began to burn in him, moving up his body until he felt his face turn red.

He couldn't wait to confront Katie Peters. Hill. Katherine Hill. Whatever her name was, she was in big trouble.

Chapter Five

As Gabe parked his Mercedes on the town square, he saw Jessica Baxter, Cal's wife, come out of The Last Roundup, carrying a little boy. He waved to her, and she hurried over.

"Gabe! It's good to see you. Cal told me you were in town."

"Yeah, good to see you, too. And this must be Rick."

Jessica grinned. "More than two seconds' acquaintance with Cal will get you that information. Cal is crazy about our baby."

Gabe played with the baby, enjoying the child's response. His shy smile was captivating. "I bet he doesn't get any attention, does he?"

Sighing, Jessica said, "Thank goodness Rick has a sweet nature, but his grandparents are even worse than Cal."

"That's the way it should be. Gran spoiled me, and I loved it."

"Sorry about her death. I know you must miss her," Jessica said, touching his arm.

"Yeah, thanks. Well, where are you headed? Want me to carry this little guy, give your arm a break?"

"I'm just going over to The Lemon Drop Shop. I need to talk to Katie about something."

"I'm heading that way, too," Gabe said, keeping his voice calm. "Let me carry Rick."

He took the little boy into his arms, surprised at how much he enjoyed his warmth.

"Thanks. He is getting heavy. Soon he'll be walking."

"Yeah, Cal brought me up-to-date on his progress."

Jessica laughed again.

"Say, Jack Ledbetter has some pups ready to sell, if you're thinking about getting him a puppy."

"Really? I hadn't thought about that, but it's a good idea. Did you buy one?"

"Yeah. I took her home before I came back to town. She's in a cardboard box with Gran's windup alarm clock and a bowl of water. I've got to buy some Puppy Chow before I go home."

"How wonderful!"

They'd reached the shop and Gabe's attention left Jessica as he looked inside the shop for Katie. "I don't see Katie—Katherine. Maybe she's gone home."

"Not Katie. She never leaves until after closing," Jessica assured him. "Why don't you sit down out here with Rick, if you don't mind, and I'll go invite her to join us. I'm going to get Rick a cookie. Do you want something?"

"No, thanks." He'd had enough of Katie's cooking today. After eating the other two sausage rolls earlier, he'd skipped lunch. Unfortunately, the thought of food had his stomach growling. Jessica laughed, which made his cheeks flush. Then she disappeared.

When she returned five minutes later, Gabe and Rick had become much closer friends. The little boy, standing in his lap, had pulled his nose, left slobbers on his shirt and bounced like a ball.

"Hey, Rick, give me a break," Gabe pleaded, smiling all the while. "I'm not a trampoline."

When the child saw his mother returning, his activity increased, especially when he spotted the cookie in her hand. "Cookie!"

"Wow, I didn't know he could talk," Gabe exclaimed.

"Only important words, like *cookie, go,* and most especially, *no.* That's his favorite."

Gabe found Jessica's chatter entertaining, but he was more interested in the result of her absence. "Where's Katie?"

"She'll be out in a minute. It's a little crowded right now."

He kept an eye on the door as they chatted. Which was why he saw Katie's face when she realized he was with Jessica. She came out carrying a tray and almost dropped it when her gaze fell on him.

"I thought—" she began, then stopped herself. "Hello, Gabe. I didn't know you were with Jessica."

"You thought she left Rick out here on his own?"

Her cheeks flushed, but Jessica intervened before Katie could answer. "She thought I meant Cal. Sorry, Katie, I didn't think about that until after I'd come back outside."

"It doesn't matter." She set a dish with a dozen cookies on it on the table. Then she put a glass of lemonade in front of each of them. "I brought the oatmeal-raisin cookies because they're Cal's favorites."

"And I appreciate that," Cal's deep voice announced. They all turned around to find the sheriff standing on the sidewalk, grinning. "I saw you from across the square and thought I'd join you." He winked at Katie. "Hoping for some of those cookies."

Jessica gave a sigh of exasperation. "Katie, I hope you don't indulge him too often. He's going to have to buy larger sizes if he eats too many cookies."

"Hey, I'm in good shape!" Cal protested, slapping his flat stomach.

With all the teasing, Gabe almost forgot the tension he'd been feeling. Almost. He watched Katie glance at him out of the corner of her eye, and he knew she hadn't forgotten anything, either.

"You talk to Gabe," Jessica ordered. "I need to talk to Katie."

"Yes, ma'am," Cal said, taking on a humble look that didn't sit well on his broad shoulders. His wife laughed at him and then turned to Katie.

"Did the triplets come today?"

Cal and Gabe didn't pretend any interest in their own conversation.

Katherine nodded, gnawing on her bottom lip. "Yes, they did."

"Well?"

"They were ready to give me a contract, but I blew it." Everyone heard the regret in her voice.

"You blew it? How? They won't find anything better than your carrot cake." Jessica's stubborn look, one Cal was quite familiar with, filled her face.

Katie patted her friend's arm. "It's okay, Jessica. I'll be fine. They wanted a discount, and I refused. I knew they might walk. But—"

"A discount? Less than I pay? That's ridiculous. You give me a rock-bottom price. You should have said you had to charge them more!" Jessica protested with heat.

Some of the tension in Katherine's shoulders left as she grinned. "Oh, Jess, you're so good to me."

"I am not." She looked at her watch. "It's not even three o'clock. I'll go call them. When I tell them—"

"No, Jess, don't do that," Katie protested. "It's a business decision. I don't think you should."

"Katie's right, baby," Cal said quietly. "I know you want to help her, but she has to do this on her own."

"Cookie!" Rick shrieked, drawing everyone's attention as he reached for the plate in the center of the table.

"No, young man," Jessica said sternly. "You've already had your cookie."

Cal leaned forward and took his first cookie. "Can't he have just one more?"

"But those have raisins in them. He might choke," Jessica warned. "I got him a butterfly cookie before."

"I'll go get him another one," Katie said, leaping to her feet.

"No, I'll go. You're on your feet all day." Jessica headed for the door to the shop. Before she went in, though, she said, "Gabe, tell Cal about the puppy." Then she disappeared.

Gabe, after a quick glance at Katie's questioning look, turned to his friend. "I bought a pup from Jack Ledbetter today. He's got three more if you're thinking about a puppy for Rick."

"Like Jericho?" Katie asked softly.

"You remember him?" Gabe asked without thinking.

"Of course. We'd just starting dating when he died," Katie replied, her gaze soft and sympathetic.

Gabe found himself leaning toward her and froze. What was wrong with him? Was he so willing to fall into her trap? No. Never. He glared at her. "That was a long time ago."

"That's a good idea," Cal said, teasing his son, trying to distract him from the oatmeal-raisin cookies. "Want a puppy, Rick?"

"Cookie!" his son informed him, a stubborn look, remarkably like his mother's, on his face.

"Will the puppy—I mean, do you have room for a dog at your place?" Katie asked.

"There's plenty of room," Gabe snapped.

"But Gran said you had a condo," she returned, frowning.

When Gabe said nothing, Cal replied for him. "But Gabe's going to be staying here in Cactus."

Katie paled. "Here?" she asked faintly.

KATHERINE HAD THOUGHT her day couldn't get much worse. She'd been wrong. Gabe was going to stay in Cactus. So she could expect to see him at any time.

She supposed she'd adjust. She had to. Her brain seemed to scramble itself whenever he came into view. With a deep sigh, she mustered a smile. "How nice."

Jessica came out with Rick's new cookie. His crowing filled the awkward silence.

Katherine thought it might be a good time to make her escape. "Glad to see all of you, but I need to—" She stopped because Gabe had grabbed her wrist in a viselike grip.

"I need to talk to you," he said, his gaze hard.

Cal picked up two more cookies and stood. "I've got to get back. Why don't you and Rick walk me over?" he asked his wife.

Jessica was staring at Gabe and Katherine. "Um, okay if—will you be all right, Katie?"

No, don't leave me! But she couldn't say that. She had too much pride to ask for protection from Gabe. Besides, he wouldn't hurt her. Much. Other than break her heart again. "Yes, of course, I'll be fine."

Gabe said nothing, watching as the other two gathered their son and waved goodbye.

When they were out of hearing, he leaned toward Katherine and she pressed against the back of her chair.

"You lied to me."

His harsh words weren't a big surprise. She'd known she'd have to pay for getting rid of him earlier today. "Not really."

"Yes, you did!" he insisted, his voice rising. "You told me you were going to marry Jack Ledbetter!"

"No, I didn't," she corrected. "I said, 'He's the one.' And he is."

He gave her a disgusted look. "I know. He's going to marry your mother. But I thought—"

"Evelyn was listening. She's a gossip."

"I wanted to talk to you in private, but you insisted on keeping her there," he pointed out.

In exasperation, near tears, Katherine said, "Gabe, I'm trying to run a business here. If I don't work, we don't eat."

"Yeah, right," he jeered. He didn't believe her. "You make plenty to put food on the table."

On a good day, she might have been able to let his comment pass. But today, with all the difficulties, with the worry that she'd blown a good opportunity, she shot back at him, "Not all of us come from a family with money. In the past few years, I've put Joe through college, Diane and Raine are still in college. Paul goes next year and Susan the year after that. I have to pay—'' She broke off, horrified that she'd said so much. She *wanted* to help her siblings. But it wasn't easy.

Jumping up from the table, she ran for the safety of her shop. Since she had surprised Gabe, she almost made it all the way to the kitchen.

But he caught her at the swinging door.

"Wait a minute!" he roared, and drew a lot of stares.

"Oh, Katherine, there's a phone call for you," Mary said as she opened the kitchen door. "I was just coming to tell you."

Katherine would have asked Mary to take a message, but the call was a good reason to get rid of Gabe. "Excuse me," she said, and wrenched her arm from his hold. Then she dashed through the swinging door.

Unfortunately, Gabe came after her.

Grabbing the phone, she gave her name.

"Mrs. Hill, this is Ron Frizzell with TGM Corporation. We visited with you earlier today."

Katherine's heart began beating double time. Was she going to get a second chance? Could fate be that kind?

"Yes, Mr. Frizzell, I remember." She held back the plea that he give her another opportunity to secure the contract. She'd wait to see what he had to say. At least she'd try to wait.

"My colleagues and I have discussed your bakery item, and we have decided to go ahead with the arrangement. We will order nine cakes a day and provide the transport for twenty-five dollars a cake. Will that be satisfactory?''

Excitement was bubbling up in Katherine and she struggled to hold on to her composure, to sound professional. "Yes, Mr. Frizzell, I accept your offer. When do you want the order to begin?"

"Today is Tuesday. Can you have the first order ready Thursday morning? That way our restaurants will have them for the weekend rush."

"Of course I can."

"Very well. Do you have a fax machine?"

"No, but my attorney's office does. Please send the papers to Alexandra Langford." Then she gave him the fax number. Mac had let her use his fax machine before.

"Very well. Payment will be mailed every Monday for goods provided through Saturday. Is that satisfactory?"

She hoped she remembered everything he told her. Her mind was racing ninety miles a minute. She even caught herself trying to calculate how much she could save before Paul started school in the fall. "Oh, yes, it's satisfactory."

"Good. Let us know if you have any difficulties."

"I will. Thank you."

When she hung up the phone and could release the excitement bursting inside of her, she spun around and discovered Gabe hovering over her, an impatient look on his face.

"Gabe! I did it! I actually did it!" she screamed, and threw her arms around his neck. Then she planted a kiss on his lips that brought the world to a halt.

GABE TOLD HIMSELF he wasn't interested in kissing Katie. He told himself he would have grabbed her and kissed her back if he hadn't been so stunned. He told himself he didn't want her more than life itself.

Impossible.

"What happened?" Mary asked from behind him. Evelyn was peering over her shoulder.

"That was one of the gentlemen who visited today," Katherine told her workers, after one darting look at Gabe. She then stepped around him. "He placed an order for nine cakes a day."

"Mercy!" Evelyn exclaimed.

Mary at once began asking questions, demanding details, and Katherine tried to answer them.

Gabe didn't feel any of the excitement showing on the three ladies' faces. But he couldn't help asking, "How are you going to produce nine cakes a day?"

"Fourteen cakes," Katherine said.

He could see the wheels turning in her head. She didn't even remember what they'd been discussing before the call came. More importantly, he didn't think she remembered that she'd kissed him.

That thought upset him more than her lie. If one kiss could destroy his peace of mind, she ought to at least remember it!

"Katherine!" he snapped. "We still need to talk."

"Gabe, I can't—"

"I won't take long."

The way she avoided looking at him made him think that maybe she did remember that kiss after all. Good.

"Ladies, we'll talk in a minute," she said quietly to the two women. They left the kitchen, staring over their shoulders at Gabe. He felt like a tiger on display.

Katherine walked away from him, circling the worktable. Putting distance between them.

He made his demand at once. "I want to know who you're seeing. You said you were seeing someone. It's obviously not Jack Ledbetter. I made a fool of myself because of your lie, but I found out the truth."

She ran a hand over the smooth cabinet, still not looking at him. "It's none of your business."

"What did you say?" He couldn't believe her response.

"I said it's none—"

"I heard your answer! Of course it's my business! If you don't marry, I'll lose my grandmother's home." He began circling the worktable. If he got close to her, he might wring her neck. Or kiss her. But that was a chance he had to take, because he wasn't going to be ignored, told it wasn't his business.

Katherine started walking again, ahead of him, rounding the opposite corner from him.

"Stop, Katie, or I'm going to get dizzy."

"I'll stop when you stop."

He came to an abrupt halt. "What's the matter? Do you think I'm going to hurt you?" He remembered his question to Cal about her husband. "Did Hill hurt you?"

She looked away. "That's none of your business, either."

Drawing a deep breath, Gabe tried to organize his thoughts. That surprise kiss had shaken him. "Look, Katie…"

"Katherine," she insisted.

He heaved another sigh. "I'm trying to remember, but old habits die hard."

An almost mournful look came over her face. "I know," she said softly, still not looking at him.

"Katie—Katherine, I have to fix this. I want to live in Gran's house, to be surrounded by her things, to feel—to remember—I don't want to lose the memories of my grandmother." He was baring his soul to her, well, some of it, anyway. She didn't deserve to know the thoughts he had of *her*.

Finally she looked at him, her beautiful blue eyes filling with tears. "Gabe, I don't know what to do. I'd help you any way I could, but I don't—"

"You'll help me?"

"But Mac said you can't break the will."

"If you'll help me, I think I can fix things." He knew he could if he could get her married to someone else. Whoever she was dating.

He ignored the empty feeling in his stomach. It was probably hunger anyway. He hadn't eaten any of Cal's cookies.

"How?"

Somehow, he didn't think she was in the mood to agree at the moment. When she wouldn't even give him a name, it didn't seem likely she'd set a wedding date. But he'd find out who the man was. He'd work from that end to encourage a wedding date. Soon.

"I'm going to have to work out the details. I'll get back to you. And Katherine, I appreciate your cooperation. That's kind of you." He gave her a smile. It wasn't sincere, or warm, or even friendly. But it was a smile.

She looked leery.

"I'll let you know what I work out, okay?"

"Yes, of course. But Gabe, I won't do anything illegal," she cautioned.

He stepped back as if she'd slapped him. "Illegal? Katherine, I'll have you know I'm a member of the bar. Do you think I'd throw away my career? Of course we wouldn't do anything illegal!"

Her smile was tremulous. She nodded. "Okay."

He turned to go, then thought of something else. "Um, I'd better warn you. I think you'll have company tonight."

Her eyes widened in disbelief. "You're coming over?"

He was almost as taken aback as she was. "No! No, not me. Jack Ledbetter. He said he was going to—he'd be over."

"Why?"

"That's none of my business," he returned, pleased to use her own excuse against her. Then he left The Lemon Drop kitchen.

Chapter Six

Katherine had a lot to do. Unfortunately, she seemed to be mired in molasses. Instead of making plans, reorganizing her kitchen, preparing for the increase in business, all she did was stare into space. Thinking about *the kiss*.

"Get over it, Katherine," she admonished herself.

It was only a kiss.

But the instant her lips had touched Gabe's, she was Katie again, that young Katie Peters, naive, optimistic...in love. Believing that her future was bright.

"Your future *is* bright. You've got a good business here. You're able to provide for your family. You're a lucky woman!" All of that was true. So why did she feel her heart had been broken all over again?

"Katherine? Did you call?" Mary asked, sticking her head past the kitchen door.

"No! No, I was thinking out loud," she assured

Mary, smiling. "Isn't that a sign of craziness, talking to yourself?"

Mary shrugged her shoulders. "I'm not going to say that, since I talk to myself all the time." After a glance over her shoulder, she said, "Things are pretty slow out here. Need some help to get ready for Thursday?"

"That would be great if Evelyn can handle business."

Mary's presence would help settle her down. Force her to concentrate on mundane matters. Make it possible to forget the taste of Gabe Dawson.

When six o'clock finally rolled around, Katherine had accomplished a lot. She'd called Jessica to give her the good news. After all, it was Jessica who had pointed out to the corporation how well her carrot cake sold. And she'd called Alex Langford to warn her about the incoming fax and ask her to review the contract for her.

She'd planned out a schedule for early mornings when she'd need more help turning out fourteen carrot cakes in addition to the cinnamon rolls and sausage biscuits. She hoped her mother would agree to come in until she found additional help.

Everything was organized.

Except her heart.

She almost dreaded going home and facing her family. Could she hide the devastation she felt? The loss all over again?

She knew she'd made the right choice ten years ago. If she'd asked Gabe to wait for her, to give her a chance to settle things with her family, he'd still be waiting. And she could never have abandoned her family.

But she'd also known he would have insisted he wait...for a while. Until he grew impatient. He hadn't been known for his patience. And the result would have been the same. Only the agony would have been prolonged.

Damn it, why did this one man have such a hold on her heart? Of course, he was handsome. But there were other handsome men. He was brilliant. Loving.

But surely there were other men with the same makeup, the same qualities. But if there were, she'd never met them. Never been interested. Never—

She clamped down on those thoughts. Concentrate on the good news. Think about telling Mom about the extra income. Watch her face light up in relief.

When Katherine reached her home, she was composed, ready to sit at the dinner table with her family and thrill them with her news. It would be a good evening. A family evening. The start of a better life.

Okay, so maybe she was exaggerating a little, but that was better than going home with her head hanging down just because of one stupid little kiss.

Then hell broke loose.

"Mom? I'm home," Katherine sang out in her most cheerful voice. Two things struck her at once. There were no enticing smells from the kitchen. And there were no noises of people moving around, going about their business.

As if to contradict that thought, her mother came running into the kitchen, tears streaming down her face, followed by Susan, making an impassioned plea.

"Tell her, Katie!" Susan screamed. "Tell her she can't do it! It's the stupidest idea I've ever heard. Tell her she can't be so selfish!"

Margaret, sobs racking her body, buried her face in her hands. She mumbled something, but Katherine had no idea what she'd said.

Katherine immediately put her arms around her mother, stroking her back. Then she turned her attention to Susan. "Calm down and tell me what you're talking about. Without any more attacks on Mom," she added in a tone of voice that let Susan know she wouldn't tolerate it.

"It's that Jack Ledbetter!" Susan spat, having found a new target for her anger.

Katherine suddenly remembered Gabe's warning as he'd left her shop. Expect company. She guessed Jack hadn't waited until evening. And now she had a clue as to the cause of Susan's anger.

She led her mother over to the table. "Where's Paul?" Her calm, supportive brother would help settle the turmoil.

"He's not home yet. He had a meeting after school. *I* had to catch a ride with Prissy Dunlap." Susan's contorted features emphasized her feeling of mistreatment. "And when I get home, I find Mom and that—that man in the living room, kissing!"

Margaret sobbed even harder, her face buried on Katherine's shoulder.

"Susan, go to your room and stay there until I've talked to Mom. And try to calm down." She and her sister dueled with stares, but Katherine won out. For ten years, she'd been the only disciplinarian in the house. Her mother wasn't strong enough to say no.

After Susan had left the room, Katherine took her mother's shoulders and eased her back, trying to see her face. "Mom? Mom, tell me what's wrong."

Her mother hiccuped several times and tried to wipe away the tears. "I wouldn't—I loved your father."

"Of course you did."

"But Jack—" She stopped and hid her face again.

"—is a wonderful man," Katherine finished.

Margaret nodded, her face flushing. "He—he wants to marry me!" she said hurriedly, shooting a guilty look over her shoulder in the direction of Susan's room.

Katherine hugged her mother. "That's wonderful. I'm so happy for you."

"But I can't marry him," Margaret said, sobbing again.

With a sigh, knowing she had an uphill battle, Katherine set out to convince her mother differently. Then she'd have to deal with Susan.

GABE WAS POURING Puppy Chow into a bowl for his new companion when he heard a vehicle outside.

Had Cal come to call again? Or one of his other friends? He stepped to the sink to look out the kitchen window. Much to his surprise, Jack Ledbetter was getting out of his truck.

''Think he's come to take you back, Cinnamon?'' he asked the puppy, curled up in the crook of his left arm. He hoped not. He was surprised at how quickly he'd gotten attached to the little dog.

A knock on the door interrupted his thoughts. He opened it for Jack Ledbetter. ''Come in, Jack. How are you?''

He blinked rapidly when the man's composure disappeared and he looked tragically at Gabe. ''I'm sorry to bother you, but I need help.''

''Come in, man. Of course, what can I do?'' In Cactus, as in most small towns, neighbors did what they could for each other. He hadn't forgotten that small-town spirit.

Gesturing to the table, he put Cinnamon back in her box and washed his hands, then poured two cups of coffee. ''What's the matter?''

Jack didn't answer at once. He gulped down coffee and tried to calm himself. ''I know this isn't any of your business, but I don't understand women too well.''

Gabe cleared his throat, hoping to hide the urge to chuckle. ''Most men don't, including me.''

''But earlier today, you gave me some advice.''

Uh-oh. Gabe immediately regretted his interference. But he hadn't thought—he'd believed Jack was talking about Katie, not her mother. "What happened?"

"I went over there—I couldn't wait until this evening. And I told Margaret how I felt. I kissed her." Jack paused, a gentle smile on his face, his eyes glazed over.

Gabe understood that reaction. After he'd made love to Katie that one time, he'd scarcely been able to think of anything else—until she rejected him.

"And she accepted?" he prodded.

His question brought Jack crashing back to reality. "No. I think she intended to. She snuggled into my arms. She fit perfectly." Another pause. "Then Susan came in."

It didn't take ESP to figure out Katie's youngest sister had spoiled the moment. "She got upset?"

Jack pressed his lips together. "It was horrible. She said terrible things to her mother. When I tried to stop her, Margaret turned on me, like a lioness protecting her cub. She told me she could never marry me."

Unhappy silence filled the room. Gabe prodded again. "And you left?"

"What else could I do? She doesn't want me." Jack was the picture of dejection.

Gabe ran his fingers through his dark hair, wondering what he should say. He and Jack might not be close friends, but they had one thing in common. They had apparently both been spurned because the Peters women were self-sacrificing. Unless Katie was telling the truth that she'd fallen for someone else.

"Look, Jack, you need to talk to Katie. I think she's in favor of you marrying her mom. She can probably help you more than I can." Gabe felt partly responsible for today's events, but there wasn't much he could do.

"I couldn't force Margaret to marry me, Gabe. She doesn't want me."

"Sounds more like Susan doesn't want you," Gabe pointed out.

"You marry a woman, you take on her family."

"What about Paul? What did he say?"

Jack sighed. "He wasn't around. Sometimes he works at Katherine's shop."

Gabe wanted to help Jack. If for no other reason than to show Katie this ridiculous behavior that seemed to run in their family was wrong. But what could he do?

Finally he got up. Scooping Cinnamon from her box, he put her in Jack's arms. "Entertain Cinnamon for me for a minute. I'll be right back."

He hurried to Gran's bedroom. The phone company was supposed to turn on the phone service today. He only hoped they'd kept their word.

No such luck. The phone was dead and he'd forgotten to charge his cell phone. So he couldn't call Katie to find out what—not what he should do, but what she and her mother wanted Jack to do. That's what he needed to discover.

He went back to the kitchen, where Jack was stroking Cinnamon, staring at the ridiculously pleased puppy.

"Jack, my phone isn't connected, so I can't call Katie. Maybe tomorrow—"

"We could go over there," Jack said, a spark of hope in his voice.

We? Gabe swallowed a sudden lump in his throat. Go to Katie's house? Face her family? "No, I don't think—"

"Please, Gabe? I know I'm asking a lot, but I won't be able to sleep tonight until things are settled. And I can't go back by myself."

Gabe stood there, staring at Jack, his mind racing, remembering the pain he'd felt. There hadn't been anyone he could talk to about Katie. No one knew they'd made love. Or that he'd proposed marriage. And been rejected.

Until he'd told Cal, he'd kept that secret, letting it fester for ten years.

He couldn't abandon Jack, not after he'd had the courage to tell someone, to seek help.

"Okay," Gabe agreed.

"You'll go with me? You'll talk to Katherine?" Jack asked, leaping to his feet. "Right now?"

Gabe reached over and took Cinnamon from Jack. The puppy had been frightened by Jack's sudden move. "Yeah, right now." He had to get it over with before he lost his nerve.

After soothing Cinnamon, he put the puppy in her box, rewound the ticking clock and turned to tell Jack he was ready.

Jack was waiting at the door.

"Susan," Katherine finally said in exasperation, "you're planning on going to college in a year, aren't you?"

"Of course I am. You know—"

"Yes, I know, but how about you stay home with Mom. After all, she'll be alone once you're gone."

"What? That's not fair! Besides, you'll be here."

Katherine felt anger rise in her and carefully tamped it down. "Did it ever occur to you that I might not always want to take care of all of you? That I might want a life of my own?"

She regretted her words at once. The stricken look on Susan's face showed how her words had affected her little sister.

"Sweetie, I'm sorry," she hurriedly said, reaching out to hug her.

Susan pushed her away. "Fine. Go. We didn't ask you to be a martyr!"

No, they hadn't asked her to turn down Gabe's offer. She'd made that choice, and she knew it was the right one. What was wrong with her today? Usually she kept her emotions in tight check. But today she'd—

"Katie?" her mother called, and Katherine heard panic in her voice.

She hurried to the door. She'd deal with Susan later. "What is it, Mom?"

"Jack! Jack is here."

"I'll be right there." She turned to look at her sister. "If you can't behave, stay in your room." Harsh words, but Susan needed to do some growing up, to think of someone other than herself.

When she got to the kitchen, the new arrival had

already come in. New arrivals. The shock of seeing Gabe behind Jack threw Katherine.

Would this day never end?

"Hello, Jack, Gabe," she said, trying to sound as if their appearance was a normal occurrence.

Jack said nothing, staring at Margaret, who was preparing dinner and keeping her gaze on the potatoes she was creaming.

Gabe cleared his throat. "Uh, Jack and I—that is, we wondered if we could visit."

"Of course. Jack knows he's always welcome here." When Gabe winced at her words, she hurriedly added, "And you, too, Gabe, even though it's been a long time." Hysterical laughter bubbled up in her. Oh, yeah, he was always welcome. Why not torture her by dropping in?

Margaret muttered something that no one heard.

"What, Mom?" Katherine asked, leaning closer.

"We have plenty of food." Margaret cast her a pleading look.

Ah. "Have you two eaten? We're running a little late tonight with dinner, but we'd be pleased if you'd join us."

Before they could answer, Paul burst in the back door. "Sorry I'm late, Mom, but—Gabe! You came to see us!"

The pleasure on her brother's face made Katherine want to cry again.

"You didn't speak to Jack," Katherine urged quietly.

"Oh, sorry, Mr. Ledbetter," Paul said, smiling

at the older man. "I was just so happy to see Gabe here."

Jack shook Paul's hand. "I understand."

"Mom's almost got dinner ready. Why don't you go wash up and, uh, tell Susan we've got company for dinner."

Paul frowned. "Why isn't Suse here helping?"

Everyone seemed to be staring at her. Katherine took a deep breath. "Just do as I asked, Paul."

After Paul left the room, Jack stepped forward. "Look, I don't want to cause you any more trouble. And if Margaret says the word, I'll leave, but I love your mother."

Margaret gasped, then started crying again.

Jack immediately crossed the room and wrapped her in his arms, trying to soothe her. Katherine looked at Gabe, wondering why he was here.

As if he read her mind, he hurriedly said, "Jack came to me, for support and advice because I'd talked to him earlier today. I actually encouraged him to go ahead and propose. But I didn't know——"

He stopped and looked away, his cheeks flushed with embarrassment.

Oh, yes. That's when he'd thought Jack was going to propose to her. He wanted her married...to someone else. Did she need any more proof that he no longer cared for her? That her kiss today only affected her?

"I see. Well, you can help set the table."

"Maybe I shouldn't stay."

She glared at him. "You're staying." After

opening the cabinet, she took six plates out and handed them to him.

With a nervous look at the couple across the room, he began placing them on the table.

Katherine joined him with silverware and napkins.

They worked in silence until the table was ready.

"Mom? Did you finish the potatoes?"

Jack looked up. "Your mother can't—"

"Yes, she can, Jack," Katherine insisted. She believed her mother would pull herself together to feed her family. And Katherine needed *someone* to stop crying. "We'll all feel better when we've eaten."

When Susan followed a tight-lipped Paul into the kitchen, Katherine only prayed she was right.

CONVERSATION WAS AWKWARD at dinner. Gabe was grateful for Paul's efforts. He and the boy talked about the local football team's last season, the baseball team's record. Jack even joined in about the baseball team. It seemed he was a baseball fan.

The three women said almost nothing.

When the meal was over, Gabe started to excuse himself. Katherine stopped him with a glare. Why did she want him to stay? It wasn't any of his business.

"Paul, do you have time to milk Betsy before you start your homework?" she asked, smiling at her brother.

"Sure," the boy agreed, and excused himself.

Then she turned to her sister. "Susan, you need to gather the eggs."

Gabe expected an explosion. The girl had been ticking like a time bomb the entire meal, growing tighter and tighter with anger.

But after a glare at her sister, Susan left the kitchen without saying anything.

He watched Katie compose herself. It was clear who was in charge of the family. Margaret Peters had done nothing to help the situation. Gabe tried to think back to the few times he'd been at their home. He hadn't paid a lot of attention to Margaret. His attention had been on Katie. It seemed to him, as he thought back, that her father had dominated the household.

"Jack," she began with a smile, "Mom and I had a long talk this afternoon. We both owe you an apology."

"No! Not at all," Jack hurriedly said, his anxious glance going to Margaret.

"Yes, we do," Katie insisted. "Susan is a teenager and thinks the world revolves around her. While I haven't convinced her yet that that's not true, I will."

"I didn't mean to upset her," Jack said, his gaze still on Margaret, a pleading look in his eyes. He was rewarded by a tiny smile from his love.

"We both know that," Katie assured him.

Gabe remembered Katie's generous nature, her sunny smile. She'd been nothing but a teenager when he'd proposed. When she'd lost her father. Yet she'd coped.

An awkward silence settled in.

Katie said, "Mom, don't you have something to say to Jack?"

Margaret shot a panicked look at her daughter. Then, as if gathering her courage, she stared at her plate. Finally, when Gabe was ready to demand she speak, she raised her head and stared at Jack. "I love you."

That ended the conversation. Jack sprang from his chair, pulled Margaret up into his arms and kissed her.

Gabe had tried to avoid all thoughts of the kiss Katie had given him earlier in the day. After all, he'd kissed other women in the past ten years. More passionately than today's kiss. Longer. With the intention of satisfying his hunger.

But they never had.

He dismissed that thought and cleared his throat.

The two older people broke apart, both flushed, and looked everywhere but at their audience.

Katie glared at Gabe. "Did you have to ruin a romantic moment?"

Anger washed through him. "No, that's your specialty. At least it was ten years ago!"

Chapter Seven

"This is not about us!" Katherine hissed, unable to believe he'd said anything about ten years ago.

"Yes, it is Because I think you did the same thing your mother is doing now."

"What's he talking about?" Margaret asked in a wavery voice.

"Nothing, Mom. Don't worry about it. Why don't you and Jack go into the living room and discuss your plans?"

"I'm talking about Katie turning down my marriage proposal," Gabe said loudly.

A loud gasp behind them had the two men turning around to discover Susan standing there with a pail filled with eggs, shock on her face. "You turned down Gabe?" she asked, horror in her voice.

Katherine stiffened her shoulders. "You needn't make it sound like I committed murder, Susan."

"Why?" Paul asked, standing behind Susan.

"Yeah, Katie, why don't you tell them? Tell them about the man you fell in love with after your dad died."

She glared at Gabe. Was the man sadistic? Why was he doing this?

Paul and Susan looked at each other, then back at her.

"I don't remember anyone," Paul said, frowning.

"Except dorky Darrell," Susan added. "But that was a couple of years later."

"Dorky?" Gabe said softly.

Katherine wanted to wring Susan's neck. Her sister had never liked Darrell. But Gabe shouldn't be looking so pleased at Susan's description of her dead husband.

Margaret spoke again. "You turned down a proposal from Gabe? When?"

Katherine refused to answer. But Gabe didn't.

"I intended to propose the weekend after your husband died, Mrs. Peters. But I waited a couple of weeks. That's when Katie told me there was someone else. At the time I believed her. Now I'm thinking she did the same thing you're doing now. Refusing to marry me because of her family."

"Gabe, that's enough!" Katherine snapped. "That's ancient history."

"I think it's time to dig up the dead bodies," he said, a determined look on his face.

"Dead bodies?" Margaret asked, puzzled.

Katherine couldn't handle any more. "Fine. But we'll do it in private. Outside!" She charged from the kitchen, not bothering to see if he followed her.

It was a peaceful night, but Katherine wasn't

calm. Life had been dull since Darrell's death, but she hadn't complained. Much.

And she never would again.

Footsteps sounded on the porch and she spun around.

"How dare you drag our personal business out in front of my family!"

"Whoa, lady. As you said, it's ancient history."

"Yes, it is! And you're right. I lied to you. It makes no difference now."

"You lied to me because you didn't think I could handle your family problems?"

"How could you, Gabe? Your parents were supporting you and you had three years of law school before you. What should I have done? Asked you to give up law school? Asked you to wait three years? Or ten years? Asked you to saddle yourself with an entire family?"

"None of those options would have hurt as much as your lie," he insisted, his jaw squaring.

"Really? You were so seriously wounded you got engaged to a beautiful woman." She tried to keep the bitterness out of her voice.

"You got married!"

But she hadn't gotten married until after she had learned of his engagement. Until after all hope was gone. But she wasn't going to say that to Gabe. If she did, he'd know the truth. That she still loved him. Had. Had still loved him then.

She didn't love him now. Not tonight. That kiss today had brought back memories, but that was all. Memories.

"And that makes this discussion unimportant. Except that now I have to go back in there and deal with my family. Thanks a lot, Gabe."

She again didn't wait for his agreement. She couldn't take any more. When she got inside, she discovered Margaret and Jack talking quietly to Paul. Susan wasn't in the room.

"Paul doesn't mind!" Margaret said, beaming at Katherine.

"Good for Paul," Katherine said, managing a smile. "Have you set a date?"

Both Margaret and Jack looked shocked.

"You think we should do that?" Jack asked.

She felt rather than saw Gabe come in, but she ignored him. "It seems the natural progression after you ask a woman to marry you," she said.

"Well," Jack started, then cleared his throat. "There'll be a lot of decisions to make. Like where we'll live, and—and the kids."

Paul shrugged his shoulders. "You don't have to worry about us. I can get a job. Tuck Langford is hiring me for the summer and I can stay on with him. I'll take care of Susan."

"What?" Katherine practically screamed. "You'll do no such thing, Paul Peters! You're going to college in the fall and don't you forget it!"

GABE WASN'T HAPPY with Katie. She'd asked him questions he couldn't answer. But he hated to see her so upset.

He stepped forward and put a hand on Paul's

shoulder. "Your sister is right, Paul. Getting your education is important."

Paul got a stubborn look on his face. "I'm old enough to—"

"We'll discuss this later," Katherine said firmly.

Jack stepped forward. "Paul, I would never separate your mother from her family. When I marry her, you and Susan and all of you become my family, too. My wife and I couldn't have children, but I wanted—I'd be happy—I'd like to help out."

Katie stepped forward and kissed the older man's cheek. Gabe was ashamed of the shaft of jealousy that shot through him.

"And that's why Mom loves you." Then she said, "We'll work out the details later, Jack. But welcome to the family."

After a quick look at his sister, Paul stepped forward and offered his hand in congratulations, too.

Jack beamed.

Gabe was sorry to end the man's pleasure, but it was time to head home. To recover from dinner at the Peters's home. "Ready to go, Jack? I need to get back to Cinnamon."

"Who's Cinnamon?" Paul asked.

Gabe wondered at the boy's concern. "The puppy I bought from Jack earlier today."

"Hey, I'd like to see him."

"Come over anytime, Paul. We've got a lot of catching up to do." He didn't mind spending time with Paul.

Jack was staring longingly at Margaret.

With a sigh, Gabe said, "Margaret, why don't

you walk Jack out to the pickup while I, uh, tell Katie something.''

The couple walked out, their arms wrapped around each other.

''What?'' Katie snapped.

''Uh, I'll say good-night,'' Paul hurriedly said, backing toward the hall door.

Katie tried to protest, but the boy disappeared.

She turned around again to stare in exasperation at Gabe. ''If you're wanting to complain again about what happened ten years ago, I don't want to hear it.''

''Nope. I wanted to give Jack a moment of privacy to kiss your mom good-night.'' He tried not to stare at her lips, to think about the kiss she'd given him earlier.

''Oh. Well, that was thoughtful of you.'' She looked away, then back at him. ''I think that's long enough, though.''

''It never was for us.''

She whirled away, but not before he saw her face flush. ''Go away, Gabe. Far, far away.'' Then she fled the room.

LYING IN BED THAT NIGHT, Gabe decided his life had gone to the dogs. A snore from Cinnamon emphasized his thought. He'd started with the puppy in its box, but every time he walked away, the puppy whimpered.

He'd moved the box into his bedroom, but that didn't satisfy Cinnamon. Now she was cuddled up against him, enjoying doggie dreams, while he stared at the ceiling.

Ah, the bachelor life. Sleeping with a dog, instead of the woman he—a woman. A beautiful woman.

He'd better put any thought of Katie out of his head. Even if he could trust her again, which he couldn't, he hurriedly assured himself, she'd made it clear tonight she felt nothing for him.

Time to take charge of his life. He would visit with the matchmakers tomorrow. They would help him find a husband for Katie. A husband who would release him from memories that seemed to hold his heart captive.

He must have fallen asleep at some point, though his body didn't feel like it, for a sharp ring woke him at daylight.

Great. They had connected his phone in time for a dawn call. He struggled out of bed, disrupting Cinnamon's sleep. The dog yipped in protest.

"Sorry, Cin. Hello?"

His mother launched into a tirade about his not calling her.

"Mom, calm down. They just connected the phone this morning. In fact, I didn't even know it was working until you called."

"And they have no other phones in that godforsaken town?" she demanded.

Gabe sighed and rubbed his face. "Mom, is there a problem? Is Dad okay?"

"Of course he is! But we wanted to know if

you've settled everything. When will you be home?''

He didn't want to tell his mother what Gran had done. She'd go ballistic. "I'm working things out. I'm not sure when I'll be home. I've still got a few days off work," he reminded her. Actually, he had the rest of the week. And he already knew he'd be in Cactus longer than that, but he wasn't prepared to tell his mother yet.

"Your father and I thought we'd go to the Bahamas for a week. We want you to come with us."

More guilt piled on Gabe. Not only was he not telling his mother the truth, but he also didn't want to go on vacation with his parents.

As she got older, his mother had become more and more demanding, running roughshod over his father and trying to do the same to him. But Gabe had put his foot down a few years back when he broke off his engagement. His mother had chosen April as her daughter-in-law and had been furious with Gabe when he'd spoiled her plans.

"I can't get away, Mom. Thanks for thinking of me, though."

She continued on for several more minutes. Finally, after demanding a promise that he would call soon, she hung up. He grabbed Cinnamon and padded into the kitchen. He'd plugged in the coffeepot last night and the enticing scent lured him on.

Several cups later, as well as some bacon and toast, he pulled out his legal pad to look at the list he'd made only yesterday morning.

Top of the list was a visit with the matchmakers.

And he should have taken care of that business first. Then he wouldn't have spent last night tending to Jack's love life.

He put a big star by number one. He could cross off number two, talk to Jack Ledbetter. He'd definitely talked more than he should have. Number three, make a decision about his job. He didn't want to think about that.

Which left number four. See Spence about a horse.

Gabe couldn't hold back a smile. Given his choice, going to Spence's ranch would come in first. But buying a horse, unless he intended to resign his job and stay in Cactus, would be ridiculous.

Immediately, he knew he'd already made his decision. He might not be able to practice law, because he wasn't going to set himself up as competition for Mac and Tuck's wife, Alex. But he'd find plenty to occupy himself with. He could ride, as soon as he bought a horse. He could hang out with the old-timers at the pool hall. He could...damn, he was going to be bored to tears without being able to practice law.

He'd wanted a break from the high pressure of his job in Dallas. But he didn't want perpetual vacation.

Heaving a sigh, he considered commuting to Lubbock. And dismissed it. Driving two hours a day didn't tempt him.

The phone rang. If it was his mother again, he was going to have the phone disconnected.

"Hello?"

"Gabe, it's Mac. Can I tempt you to lunch at The Last Roundup?"

Pleasure filled him. "You bet. I don't have anything scheduled."

"Great. I've got an idea I think you might like. See you at eleven. We'll beat the noon rush."

"See you then."

He checked his watch and realized he could make a trip to Spence's ranch before lunch. It was only eight-thirty. The day was looking up.

KATHERINE'S DAY didn't start well.

When she met her mother in the kitchen at five-thirty, before the sun was up, Margaret seemed to be lost in her own world. A very pleasant world, judging by the smile on her lips.

"Mom, I didn't get to tell you my news last night."

"Yes, dear."

"I got a contract to supply nine more carrot cakes daily for restaurants in Lubbock."

"Yes, dear."

"I think it means we'll have the money for Paul's tuition next fall, plus a little extra to start saving for Susan's." She expected her words to finally pierce the haze around Margaret.

"Yes, dear."

In frustration she watched as her mother stirred sugar into the eggs she'd beaten. Things were not going well.

"Mom!"

Her sharp voice had Margaret turning to stare at her. "Is something wrong?"

"You just sugared the eggs."

Margaret stared at the bowl in front of her as if it had sprouted wings. "I did?"

Katherine put her arm around her mother. "I know you're distracted, what with last night's events, but I'm going to need your help at the shop in the morning. Can you come?"

"Why? Is Evelyn or Mary sick?"

With a sigh, Katherine started her story all over again.

She'd almost finished eating breakfast, her mother having agreed to her request, when Susan stumbled into the kitchen. Not a morning person, Susan usually had to be dragged from her bed to get to school on time.

"Susan!" Katherine exclaimed. "Is something wrong? Are you sick?"

"No! I'm fine. I thought I'd help Mom with breakfast. Uh, want me to gather eggs this morning, too? I think they're laying more now."

Katherine and her mother looked at each other, but it was to Susan that Katherine spoke. Standing, she hugged her sister. "Thanks, angel, but we'll need them tomorrow. I got a new contract yesterday. It'll mean extra money for college."

Again her announcement met with no enthusiasm.

"I'm thinking about getting a job."

"I thought you were going to work for me this summer. I'm counting on you."

"You don't need me. You're giving me a job because I'm your sister. Well, I'll save you some money. I'll get a job at the Dairy Queen." Her statement was accompanied by a sniff.

Katherine wanted to groan. To cover her face with her hands and ask "Why me?" Instead, she smiled at Susan. "With this new contract, I have to have someone. If you hate the idea of the job, then I'll find someone else. But I'd rather have you."

Susan gave her a cautious look. "Are you sure? Because I don't want you to make any more sacrifices."

Katherine wanted to kill Gabriel Dawson.

"Oh, yeah, I'm sure. We're going to be making fourteen carrot cakes six days a week. You'll be busy."

The high number awed Susan into forgetting her martyr posture. "Wow. That's awesome. How did that happen?"

"Jessica put in a good word for me."

"It happened because your sister is an excellent cook and a hard worker," Margaret said, adding her own explanation.

Susan slumped. "I've tried to help. I can't help it if I'm a night person."

Katherine gave her sister another hug. "Mom wasn't complaining about you, Suse. You've been a good helper. And you'll work your buns off this summer," she added with a smile.

Susan threw back her shoulders and gave a brave smile, as if she were being sent into battle. "I'll be there for you, Katie. I promise."

"Good. I have to run. See you this evening."
She hurried out the door, reminding herself that if
Gabe came within sight today, she was going to let
him have it.

GABE WAS THE PROUD OWNER of a good-looking
gelding by the time he got to the restaurant. And a
sweet little bay mare.

Before he'd left the ranch, Spence had teased him
about the purchase of the mare. She was a little too
lightweight for him to ride.

"Who's gonna be riding Daisy?"

"I don't know, Spence. I don't want Thunder to
get lonesome."

Spence grinned. "I thought maybe you had a
lady friend from Dallas who might be visiting
you."

"Nope. I'm done with the big city. At least for
a while."

"Hot dog! It'll be like old times. We rodeo on
Saturdays, you know. Can you still hang on to a
horse like you used to?"

"Maybe," Gabe said with a smile. "I'm not sure
about surviving those times I don't hang on. My
bones are getting old."

Spence had slapped him on the back and offered
words of encouragement.

As Gabe entered the restaurant, he was remembering when he'd taught Katie to ride. Her parents
hadn't been able to afford any horses. But his
grandmother always kept horses for him. Their last
summer together, he and Katie had gone for long

rides, holding hands. Picnicking under the few shade trees. Even wading in the creek.

"Gabe, back here," Mac called, catching his attention.

Surprise filled Gabe as he realized Mac wasn't alone.

Not only was his partner, Alexandra Langford, sitting at the table, but also a man Gabe didn't know.

The men stood, and Mac gestured to the other man. "Gabe, let me introduce Rick Astin."

Gabe automatically held out his hand, but as he did, the name came into focus. "CAP computers?"

"Used to be," the man said, a smile on his face. He was dressed in typical Cactus gear, jeans, boots and a flannel shirt.

"You live here?" Gabe asked in surprise.

"Yeah. I have the spread between Tuck and Spence."

"Oh. The old Miller place."

"Yeah."

Gabe had noticed someone with money must have bought it, because the fencing was new and expensive, with a gate that meant business.

The waitress appeared at once and they all ordered. As soon as she'd left the table, Mac leaned forward. "I asked Rick to meet with us because he's considering hiring us on a retainer."

Gabe looked at the other man. "You expecting a law suit?"

Rick grinned. "Nope. But I'm starting a couple of new companies."

"Here in Cactus?" Gabe knew what new businesses could mean to a town the size of Cactus.

"Yeah. Here and in Fort Worth."

"Well, I couldn't recommend anyone more than Mac and Alex."

"I agree," Rick assured him. "Mac's already helped on a personal matter."

Gabe wasn't sure what was going on, but he didn't think Mac had asked him to lunch to help him persuade Rick to hire his firm. So why had he brought them together?

Chapter Eight

Mac grinned, as if realizing Gabe's confusion. "You're here because we're going to need some help. Another lawyer."

Gabe's heartbeat sped up. Was this the answer to his future? Could he live here in Cactus *and* have a law career?

"You expect that much work?" he asked cautiously. No need to get his hopes up unduly.

It was Alexandra who answered. "There will be an increase in work and both of us are already working more than we intended." She smiled. "You know Mac doesn't need the money, and, frankly, neither do I. And I'm expecting our second child in six months."

"Congratulations," Gabe said, smiling back. "Wow, Tuck with *two* babies. Incredible."

Mac looked superior. "I'm ahead of him. I already have two."

Rick's grin was even bigger. "Got you both beat. I have two with a third on the way."

Then all three of them stared at Gabe. He raised

both hands in protest. "Hey, don't look at me. I'll be the resident bachelor. Someone has to be."

"Not in Cactus," Alexandra assured him. "That's like painting a target sign on your chest."

"I'll duck," Gabe told her. And reminded himself that he had to visit the matchmakers today. He intended to paint a target sign, all right, but not on himself.

"So what do you think?" Mac asked, leaning forward. "I know you said you hadn't made up your mind yet about staying, but I thought you should know about the opportunity."

"Actually, I have made up my mind." He paused, then said, "I bought some horses from Spence this morning. I'm staying."

"Yahoo!" Mac whooped, clinching his fist in the air. "All right, Gabe. That's great!"

"That doesn't mean he'll want to work with us," Alexandra said quietly. "Some men have difficulty working with a woman."

Gabe shook his head. "I'm not one of them. I like the people I work with to be smart. And that's already a guarantee or Mac wouldn't be working with you. I'd be delighted to buy into the partnership, or simply work for the two of you."

Mac gave Alexandra a "see, I told you so" look. Then he turned to Rick. "You have any questions about Gabe's experience? Want him to tell you what he's been doing?"

"Actually, I would." Rick gave him a smile, but he waited for Gabe's reply.

Gabe summed up his experience in Dallas after graduating in the top quarter of his law school.

"Sounds like your experience will complement Mac and Alex's. You'll be the best firm in north Texas."

After they ate, Rick excused himself. "I don't like to leave Megan alone too long." After shaking hands, he hurried out.

"She's not really alone," Alexandra said with a smile. "Her mother lives with them and they have a lot of employees, but he's crazy about Megan."

"Another matchmaker success," Mac added.

"The matchmakers put them together?" Gabe asked, his interest quickening.

"Yeah. Megan and her mom had just moved back. Her mom was raised here and knew our mothers. Megan thought, and I advised, that it would be best if she were married. She was trying to get guardianship of her sister's two children. None of us knew Rick was wealthy. He was working his place almost by himself, on a tight budget."

"Why?" Gabe asked, wondering if the guy was crazy. He'd heard the computer company sold for over a billion dollars.

Mac shrugged his shoulders. "He wanted to prove himself, to...to get involved in life again."

He didn't have to say any more. While Gabe didn't have a billion dollars, he had a lot of money now. But he'd felt lost, unanchored.

"Sounds like he's doing good things for Cactus."

"Yeah. So, do you want to be a partner? Alex

and I talked about it, and we're both happy with that idea. But if you don't want the responsibility, we're okay with that, too.''

Gabe looked at first Mac and then Alex. "I'd like to be a partner.''

After lingering over coffee, working out the details, Gabe left his two new partners and started toward his car. His gaze automatically went to The Lemon Drop Shop.

And he came to an abrupt halt.

There, at an outside table, sat the four women he needed to talk to.

Mabel Baxter, Cal's mother, Edith Hauk, Spence's mother, Ruth Langford, Tuck's mother, and Florence Greenfield, Mac's aunt. All four ladies were sitting at a table under one of the yellow umbrellas.

Fate was with him.

He crossed the square and headed straight for their table, after making a quick visual check for Katie. She wasn't in sight.

All four ladies greeted him enthusiastically. After all, he'd played with their sons often.

"I hope you don't mind me intruding," he said. "But I've been hoping to visit with you.''

"We're delighted you're joining us. Pull up another chair," Mabel invited.

Gabe did as she asked.

Florence leaned forward. "Katie will bring you out a lemonade if you ask. Or some cookies.''

Gabe tried to control his nerves as he looked over

his shoulder. "Uh, no. I just ate, with Mac and Alex, and a new guy, Rick Astin."

Ruth nodded, smiling. "Rick is so nice. He's doing a lot for Cactus."

"I heard. Actually, I'm joining Mac and Alex's law firm," Gabe said, a little surprised at how good that announcement felt to him. He'd had bigger successes in his career, but this connection pleased him.

After a round of congratulations, the ladies turned the discussion to their favorite subject, asking Gabe about his romantic situation.

"Actually, that's what I wanted to talk to you about," he began.

Edith cut him off before he could continue. "You want some help getting back with Katie? That's wonderful!"

"No!" Gabe roared, standing.

The ladies all stared at him curiously, and he turned beet red as he subsided back into his chair. "I mean, I want you to find someone *else* for Katie to marry."

"Katie wants to marry? Of course, we'd be delighted to help her," Florence said, her voice softening. "She's such a wonderful person."

"We'll talk to her," Mabel said. "I'm sure she's shy about—"

"No!" Gabe took a deep breath. He couldn't believe his lack of control. "Uh, Katie doesn't—she's not planning on remarrying, but—hell!—I mean, Gran left me her estate on the condition that I marry Katie."

There. The truth was out. He knew the ladies would help him now. But they were all staring at him as if he'd lost his mind.

"And you want her to marry someone else?" Mabel asked.

He drew a deep breath. "I forgot to mention that I don't have to marry her if she marries someone else first."

"So you're not interested in Katie any longer?" Edith asked. "Because you used to be—"

"No, I'm not."

"No, he's not," a soft voice said behind him. He spun around in his chair, almost tipping it over, to find Katie standing behind him.

KATHERINE HAD KEPT her eye out for Gabe all morning. But she hadn't expected to find him sitting at one of her tables, surrounded by old friends.

Nor had she expected to hear him disavow any interest in her. Not that it was a shock. He'd made it pretty clear he wasn't interested in having anything to do with her once he got his inheritance.

"How nice of you to share your lack of interest with the town," she added, staring at him.

"I didn't mean—I was trying to explain—" Gabe began, his cheeks red.

"I think you've explained enough. Did you want something to drink?"

"No."

"Ladies, can I bring you more cookies, or refill your drinks?"

"No, thank you," Mabel said with a smile. "But

I heard a rumor this morning about your mother. Is it true?''

"Why don't you ask Gabe? He's almost as good as the four of you. Mom owes it all to him." And she hurried back into the shop. Let Gabe be grilled by those women for every detail. It would serve him right.

She went past Evelyn, at the counter, to the kitchen. There was usually a lull in business until three or four, so she needed to use the time to prepare for the morning. She took a crisper filled with carrots and set them down by the cutting board. Then she picked up a large knife.

She began to methodically lop off the ends of the carrots. It took a lot of them to make fourteen carrot cakes. Just as she was bringing the knife down on the last of the carrots, Gabe burst into the kitchen.

"Katie!"

She jerked and came close to losing a finger. With a scream, she dropped the knife.

"You cut yourself?" Gabe asked, horror in his voice as he reached for her.

She slapped at his arm, moving back. "No, no thanks to you. How dare you come into my kitchen, scaring me like that!"

Both Evelyn and Mary appeared in the door. "Are you all right?" they both asked.

"I'm fine. Nothing's wrong."

After staring at both Gabe and Katherine, the two women withdrew.

"Get out of my kitchen," Katherine muttered without looking at him.

"I need to talk to you."

"No, you don't. You've done more than enough, especially when it comes to me and my family."

"You aren't happy about Jack and your mom?"

"Of course I'm happy about them. But I'm not happy that Susan now sees herself as a martyr."

"What are you talking about?"

"Since she thinks I sacrificed myself for her, she feels she must suffer for me. Thanks to you."

"It's true."

"How do you know it was a sacrifice? We might have been horrible together. Your mother hated me and you—"

Gabe looked shocked. "What?"

"Oh, please, Gabe, everyone in town knew your mother had no intention of letting you waste yourself on a country girl with no education." Everyone but Gabe. She'd loved how he ignored his mother's attitude.

"That's not true. Mom may not have thought you were right for me, but she didn't hate you." He was frowning, as if remembering the past.

She shrugged. "It doesn't matter. Just go. I've got a lot to do."

"Did you ever make it to college?"

She closed her eyes to hide her pain. Of all the things she'd given up when her father died, most important, second to Gabe, was her dream of going to college. That was why she was so determined that her brothers and sisters get their education.

Joe had graduated two years ago and was working for Texas Instruments in Dallas. But next weekend he was coming back to town to interview with Rick Astin, hoping to work in Cactus.

Diane was in her last year at Texas Tech's law school. Raine would begin her senior year at Tech next fall. And then there was Paul and Susan.

"No, except for a couple of business classes."

Once she'd started her shop, there hadn't been time for classes. She'd been too busy trying to make a living for her family.

"If you married, your husband might be able to help with some of your responsibilities."

She whirled around to glare at him. "You think I'd do that? Lure some unsuspecting man into paying my way? Thanks, Gabe. That tells me what you think of me!"

"No! But look, I heard your husband wasn't much help, so I can—"

"Don't say anything about Darrell! He may not have been the best husband in the world, but it wasn't all his fault. He didn't deserve—" she stopped, trying to hold back the tears.

"What?" Gabe asked fiercely. "He got to marry you! I think he was a pretty lucky guy who treated you shabbily." He grabbed her arm and turned her to face him. "Tell me why I should feel sorry for a drunk who killed himself."

She hadn't intended to say anything. Ever. "He loved me! He thought he could make me love him, but he couldn't! So you see, he didn't feel so lucky to be married to me!"

She slapped a hand over her mouth too late. She'd never told anyone why she felt so guilty about Darrell. Not that she hadn't told him that she didn't love him before she accepted his proposal. But he'd thought she'd change.

She'd tried. After hearing about Gabe's engagement to a beautiful, sophisticated woman, she'd figured she'd be an old maid the rest of her life. But Darrell had offered her a chance to have a normal life. To end those lonely nights. To maybe even have babies of her own.

Instead, she'd been lonelier than ever.

"If you didn't love him, why did you marry him?" Gabe asked roughly.

She didn't want to answer that question. "That's none of your business. I asked you to leave the kitchen." She kept her gaze on his flat stomach, unable to look at him.

"When did you marry?"

Another question she didn't want to answer.

"I was twenty-one. Old enough to know better." She tugged against his hold, but he didn't let her go.

"That's the year I got engaged."

No kidding.

"You haven't asked why I broke my engagement."

"That's none of *my* business."

"You sure like that expression," he said.

She took a quick glance and was surprised to see him smiling. Some of the tension left her. She hated fighting with Gabe. "It can't be because she was ugly. I heard she was an ex-model."

"Yeah. A blonde, like you, but kind of plastic."

"Then why did you get engaged?"

"That's none of your business," he said, his smile growing.

She acknowledged his teasing with a return smile. "True."

"I think the main reason I broke it off is she couldn't kiss as good as you."

Her gaze snapped to his face, and her eyes widened in surprise. But she didn't have long to look. His lips closed the distance and covered hers in a demonstration of the magic that happened when they kissed. It had always been that way. The small taste she'd gotten the other day had only been a brief reminder, nothing compared to this invasion.

She lost all awareness of time or place. Instead, she was in the timeless heaven of Gabe's arms.

"Katherine?" Mary began, as she entered the kitchen. "Do you want—oh! Oh, excuse me! I thought—"

Gabe freed her and stepped back.

Katherine stared at him, having difficulty coming back to reality.

"I'll go, like you asked."

Sure. *Now* he agreed to go, after turning her world upside down. She stared as he turned and walked away.

"I'm sorry," Mary began, but Katherine ignored her.

She couldn't let him go. Not without asking him—not without at least saying something. He was already at the shop door when she came out of the kitchen. Instead of calling his name, she hurried after him.

Opening the shop door, she almost ran into his back. He'd stopped when Mabel Baxter called to him.

"Gabe! Come on over. I think we've figured out the perfect man for Katherine to marry so you'll be off the hook."

GABE HAD LOST his concentration about the time his lips covered Katie's. All that talk about their kisses had made it impossible to resist the temptation. If Mary hadn't interrupted them, he might not have been able to stop. That's why he'd decided to get the hell out of there. He wasn't ready to offer his heart up on a platter.

Not again.

But he wasn't ready to think of Katie with another man, either. "What?"

"You know, dear, you asked us to find some man for Katie to marry so—oh, hi, Katie." Mabel's voice reflected her embarrassment.

Gabe whirled around to find Katie staring at him, her cheeks pale, desolation in her gaze.

"Katie," he began, reaching for her, but she didn't wait to hear what he had to say.

She whirled and ran back into the shop.

This time he didn't dare follow her.

Mabel plucked at his sleeve. "I'm sorry, Gabe, but I didn't see her behind you."

"Yeah," he muttered. He didn't know what else to say. He couldn't say it was all right.

"Well, we did come up with someone. There's a rancher east of town with four little children. He needs a mother for them in the worst way. Katie—"

"No! She's already had to raise her brothers and sisters. Don't you think she should get a few years off for good behavior?" He remembered her face when he'd asked if she'd gone to college. His heart ached for her lost dreams. "No one with kids!" he snapped.

"Really, Gabe, we didn't know you'd be so difficult," Mabel protested.

"I think Gabe's right," Florence said, standing. She came over to pat his arm. "There's the minister, a very nice man. Katie would make an excellent minister's wife, she's so patient and well liked."

"No, I don't want—" Gabe stopped, frustrated, and ran his hand through his hair. "Damn it! Isn't there some man who would let Katie be Katie? Who would help her? She deserves—the best!"

"Well, of course she does," Edith said. "I told them that, but they argued with me."

He nodded eagerly at Edith. "Yeah. Who did you think would do for Katie?"

"Ruth and I are in agreement about the best man for Katie. But the other two said no."

"Who?" Gabe asked again. He wasn't going to marry Katie off to just anyone.

"Why, Gabe, dear, the perfect man is you."

Chapter Nine

Gabe opened the oven door and stared at the steak sizzling there. Not that he wanted another steak. That's what he'd eaten at lunch. But it was the easiest thing to cook.

His baked potato was in the microwave. He could cut up a salad, but it didn't seem worth the effort.

Nothing seemed worth the effort tonight. After walking away from Katie, from the best kiss he'd had in ten years, he'd had to face what he'd done. He'd asked the matchmakers to find her another man.

Damn! That's what he needed. Katie married to someone else. That way he'd inherit Gran's estate and...and he wouldn't have to be afraid he'd lose his heart to Katie again.

He was a coward.

Okay, so he knew that.

Cinnamon whined and Gabe absentmindedly bent to pet her even as he considered his situation.

Was it fair to force Katie into marriage with another man to save his own bacon? Not that he could really force her, but he could tempt her. He could let the ladies do what it appeared they did best.

The phone distracted him. With a frown, he turned off the broiler and crossed the room to the phone.

"Hello?"

"Darling, what have you done?"

"Hi, Mom. What have I done?"

"You've quit your job! I couldn't believe it when Mr. Danforth called to tell us."

"Why would he call to tell you?"

Silence. He waited, saying nothing.

"Well, actually I called his secretary to find out when you'd be back in the office," she finally admitted. "I was worried about the way you sounded this morning. He called me back a few minutes ago."

"And you called to congratulate me?" He knew better, but he wasn't happy with his mother. He was tired of her attempts to manipulate him.

"Don't be absurd. Why would I congratulate you on giving up an excellent position in Dallas to live in that little backwater town of Cactus? It took me twenty-two years to get your father out of there."

"Is Dad there? I'd like to talk to him." He figured his father might be happy for him. Now that he thought about it, he didn't think his father had been happy since he left Cactus.

Another silence. Finally his mother said, "No, he's not here. I sent him to the store for something."

"Have him call me when he gets in." Then he

hung up the phone. He'd never acted so rudely to his mother. But he didn't like her checking up on him. And he had been remembering all afternoon his mother's behavior when he was dating Katie. Katie's words about his mother had forced him to think about the past. Several conversations with the matchmakers confirmed his fears.

Fifteen minutes later, halfway through his steak, the phone rang again. This time when he answered, he heard his father's voice.

"Dad, how are you?"

"Fine, son, as usual. And you?"

"I'm doing much better. I'm going to stay in Cactus, Dad, and live in Gran's house. I'm committed to becoming a partner in Mac Gibbons's law office."

"Is that what you want?"

Gabe could hear some fierce whispering, knowing his mother was at his father's elbow. "Yeah, Dad, it's exactly what I want. I'd gotten tired of the rat race. I just hadn't admitted it because I didn't think I could practice law here. I would never compete with Mac."

Another tussle distracted him. Then his mother's voice intruded into their conversation.

"Gabe Dawson, you come home at once. I won't let you make such a mistake. Why, you might as well tell me you're marrying that little hick! I won't stand for it."

Gabe held the phone to his ear, but his mind was traveling back ten years. No wonder Katie hadn't asked him to wait for her, or asked him to help her with her family. He could thank his mother for her giving up on him. And himself, too, for being so self-absorbed.

"I haven't told you about Gran's will, have I, Mom?"

"Didn't she leave you everything?" she asked sharply.

His father had always been a good provider, but it never seemed to be enough. His grandmother had told her son years ago that she would leave everything to her grandson. Gabe's mother had been furious.

"Sort of. There were conditions. And one of them concerned that little hick, as you called her."

"No! Don't get close to her. April and I will be out to visit with you. She'll convince you to come back."

"You've been in contact with April?"

"She's never married, dear. She loves you. She's been very patient, waiting for you to realize she's the one."

Which meant, of course, that no one else with any money had come along.

"Forget it, Mom. Put Dad back on the phone."

"No! No, I won't have you destroy my dreams!" she shrieked.

He hung up on his mother for the second time in his life.

He couldn't destroy all *her* dreams? He realized how many decisions he'd made based on his mother's opinion. And none of them had made him happy.

It was time to make some changes.

He shared the rest of his steak with Cinnamon. *She* wasn't complaining about his behavior.

KATHERINE WAS MORE TIRED than she could remember being after a day at the shop. She hadn't done that much more. No, her weariness stemmed from the emotional trauma of Gabe's visit.

"It's your own fault," she muttered. After all, she'd let herself hope. A ridiculous thing to do. But when he'd taken her into his arms, of his own free will, and kissed her as he once had, as if she meant everything in the world to him, her heart had soared.

Only to crash.

She should have known better. Her hopes must have been plastered all over her face. And Gabe Dawson had always been a man with a healthy appetite.

Never again.

The issue between them was about money. She wouldn't forget that. After all, she should have expected it. He was his mother's son. And that woman had a calculator for a heart.

Jack was sitting in the kitchen when she got home, watching her mother work with a bemused smile on his face.

"Evening, Katherine. Your mom invited me to supper."

"Of course she did, Jack. And I'm glad. We always eat better when you're coming," Katherine told him, grinning at her mother when she spun around to protest.

"Are the kids home?" she asked, before either of them could say anything.

"Yes," Margaret said, frowning. "Susan didn't even have to be reminded to collect the eggs."

Katherine shook her head, chuckling. "Don't worry about it. After a few days, we should have the old Susan back. Hopefully, a little nicer, but almost the same. I'm going to wash up. Then I'll come set the table."

She entered her bedroom and looked around her. When Paul went away to college, she'd like to make his room her office. Now her room was cluttered with her paperwork. At least she had her own bedroom.

While all the kids had been at home, they'd shared rooms. When Diane and Raine occasionally came home, she and Susan again had roommates.

It suddenly occurred to her that if Jack moved into the house with her mother, and everyone got along, she might be able to get her own place. It was an added expense, an unnecessary expense, of course, but she wasn't going to be a martyr.

For the first time since she'd realized today that Gabe really didn't want her, her spirits brightened. Finding time alone was next to impossible right now. But if she had her own place, an apartment on the square—she warned herself not to get too caught up in the idea. A million things could make it impossible.

When she reached the kitchen again, she found the table already set.

"Susan came in and set the table?" she asked.

"No, Jack did," Margaret announced, pride in her voice.

"She wouldn't let me do anything else," he said with a shrug. "But I do know how to set a table."

"You did a great job, Jack. Thanks. Want to help me put ice in glasses for us?"

While they were doing so, Susan and Paul came in the back door.

"We've got a dozen more eggs than usual, Katie," Susan announced, holding up the bucket she used to gather the eggs.

"Good. We'll need them for the new orders. Did you and Mom and Paul work everything out for the morning? You can't turn over and go back to sleep."

"I know!" Susan said sharply.

Aha. Martyrdom was wearing thin. Katherine gave her sister a sympathetic pat, then handed her two glasses of iced tea to carry to the table.

"Oh, Katie," Margaret suddenly said. "Joe called today. He's flying in tomorrow night. Can we pick him up at the airport?"

"Of course, Mom. What time's his flight?"

"Eight o'clock," her mother said as she carried a platter of chicken-fried steak to the table.

Katherine would barely finish work before she had to come home, pick up her mother and make the hour drive into Lubbock. Then, after the drive home, she'd fall into bed to start her day only a few hours later.

"Say, why don't I take you to dinner in Lubbock, pick up Joe and bring him back home?" Jack asked. Then he turned a bright red. "Unless—that is, I don't want to horn in on anyone's—I mean, I guess it's a family thing."

Katherine spoke before anyone else could. "I think that's a lovely idea. Mom has to eat her own cooking all the time. It will be a treat for her and save me some time and energy."

Susan opened her mouth, but Katherine stared at her, daring her to complain. She looked away and said nothing.

"Then, when you get back, with Joe, we can all visit."

"Yeah," Paul chimed in. "That will give us time to get our chores done before Joe gets here. Good idea, huh, Susan?"

He seemed surprised when his sister glared at him. He was such an innocent. Katherine worried about him going off to college on his own.

"Well, let's eat," she said, filling the awkward silence that followed. "Did Joe say anything about his interview?"

"Just that he'd be talking with Mr. Astin himself. I wish I had the nerve to call him," Margaret said.

"Call Joe?" Paul asked.

"No, Mr. Astin. To try to persuade him to hire Joe."

"Don't worry, Mom," Katherine assured her. "Joe's credentials will get him the job. He's good."

"Yes, I suppose you're right," Margaret agreed with a sigh.

They all sat down to eat.

BY THE NEXT MORNING, Gabe had decided to call his father at work. He was going into town to look at the space available in Mac and Alex's offices, try to organize an area for his work space. He'd need to go back to Dallas to pack his things. Unless his father would do it for him.

"Dad? Sorry to bother you at work."

"No problem. I'm sorry for your mother's behavior last evening."

Gabe heard a sad acceptance in his father's voice. It occurred to him that he'd be sounding the same way had he married April. Because they would now have one child, as his mother had, and he'd never abandon his son or daughter. As his dad had refused to do.

Suddenly a lot of things were clear.

"Dad, you don't have to stay with her for me anymore."

A long silence followed his words.

Then his father sighed. "Strangely enough, at one time I loved her."

"I'm staying in Cactus. You're welcome to join me."

"And do what? Twiddle my thumbs? I'm almost sixty. It's too late to start a new career."

Gabe's heart ached at the weary resignation in his father's voice.

"It's because of her that Gran left everything to me, isn't it?"

"We both agreed it would be for the best."

"Dad, I've made a lot of money. We'll have enough. And we can buy a herd of cows. You can operate the place again. And the beauty of it is, Mom won't come near Cactus, much less a cow."

Another silence.

"I'll think about it," his father finally said.

"While you're thinking, would you be willing to find someone to pack up my office and my condo? List the condo for sale and ship everything here? I really don't want to come back to Dallas."

"Your mother's not that scary," his father said with a wry chuckle.

Gabe laughed, feeling better than he had in a while. Just as he was about to hang up, he thought of one more question. "Dad, do you have anything against Katie?"

"Katie Peters? Not at all. But your grandmother said she got married."

"Yeah, but she's widowed now. Gran left her estate to me on the condition that I marry Katie."

"What?" his father demanded, sounding stunned. "But how could she do that to you?"

"She left me an out. If Katie marries someone else before a year is up, I get the estate anyway."

"And if that doesn't happen?"

"Half of it goes to Katie, and the other half to charity."

"I can't believe my mother did that."

Gabe gave a quiet chuckle. "I couldn't, either. But I'm beginning to think she wasn't crazy after all."

KATHERINE BREATHED a sigh of relief. The final six cakes were in the oven, almost done. And it was only eight o'clock. They'd have time to cool and be iced before the delivery man arrived at nine-thirty.

"Are there any more sausage rolls?" Mary called from the kitchen door. "We're having a run on them this morning."

Margaret turned around. "I'm taking out the last two pans now. I'll bring them out."

Katherine stepped over and hugged her mother. "You've been such a help, Mom. I promise I'm going to look for someone else to work mornings right away."

"No need for that. I can do it."

Katherine shook her head. "Nope. You're going to be busy planning a wedding."

Her mother's cheeks flushed and her gaze grew dreamy again. Katherine grabbed the oven mitt and removed the pans of sausage rolls from the oven. "I'll take these out to Mary. You watch those cakes. We can't afford to let them overcook."

When she entered the shop, she realized Mary hadn't been kidding. They were crowded. She placed the rolls on the shelf behind the counter and began waiting on customers. Evelyn didn't come in until nine, so she and Mary were on their own for a while.

"Good morning, Rev. Brewster," she said,

greeting the next in line. "You're not a frequent customer. What brings you in today?"

"There's a ladies' auxiliary meeting at the church, and Mabel Baxter asked me to pick up some of your cinnamon rolls. I think it's called bribery," he said, lowering his voice and grinning.

"Whatever works," she responded with a smile. "How many do you need?"

"A dozen?"

Katherine got a box and filled it with warm cinnamon rolls. "Anything else?"

"No, I think that will bankrupt our expense account for the week," he told her, still smiling.

"Then why don't I make a donation? They're on the house."

"No, no, I couldn't do that."

"Please, Rev. Brewster, I'm delighted."

"All right...if you'll promise to call me Tony." The customer behind the reverend cleared his throat and Katherine realized it was Gabe. "Anything else, Tony?" she asked pleasantly, ignoring Gabe's glare.

"No, thanks, Katie," the reverend said, moving away, leaving her to face Gabe.

She'd planned to avoid Gabe. She'd determined last night that thinking about him would be a foolish thing to do.

"May I help you with anything?" she asked him, keeping her voice emotionless.

"You shouldn't be so friendly with the reverend," he said in a low voice. She blinked at him in surprise, anger building in her. Then, she looked over his shoulder. "Good morning, Mrs. Hambrill. What can I get for you?"

"I'm next," Gabe protested.

"What did you want?"

"A couple of sausage rolls and a cup of coffee."

Briskly she served him and took his money. When she turned to ring him up, he muttered, "Keep the change."

"No! Here it is, sir."

He glared at her. "Why so formal?"

"Now, Mrs. Hambrill, did you want your usual?" she asked, ignoring Gabe.

After glaring at her again, he moved over to a small vacant table.

"Oh, yes, please. I'm going to start my diet tomorrow, so I thought I'd have a cinnamon roll and orange juice today."

Doc and Florence Greenfield were her next customers. They were accompanied by a stranger.

"Hi," Katherine greeted them.

"Morning, Katie," Doc said cheerfully. "We've got a visitor and want him to taste the best cinnamon rolls in Texas. And the sausage rolls, too."

"You're just in time, Doc. We're about to run out. How many?"

After she'd filled their order, they grabbed the last table inside, right next to the small one Gabe occupied.

After the line disappeared, Katherine picked up a carafe of coffee and toured the room, filling cups. Their regular customers usually got up and filled their own, but Katherine would do so when she could.

Gabe held out his cup. "Why don't you join me?" he suggested.

"No, thanks." After filling his cup, she moved on, but she could feel him staring at her.

Doc asked her the same question. But instead of refusing, she pulled up another chair. "I just have a minute. I've got Mom in the kitchen helping out."

"Really? Is she going to work here now?" Doc asked. Since he and Florence had lived here as long as her mother, they were all friends.

"No, not when I find someone else. Do you know of anyone who would like an early-morning shift, Florence?" Both as the doctor's wife and a long-time member of the community, Florence would have the answer to her need.

"Hmm, I might. There's a lady whose husband works a night shift in Lubbock. He gets in about five. If he'd be willing to get the kids off to school, I think she could use the money. Ethel Moore," she added, naming the woman, and Katherine remembered meeting her.

"If I can interrupt you two women discussing business," Doc said, smiling, "I'd like to introduce our friend." He motioned to the man beside him.

"A very happy friend, I might say," the man said with a nod toward Katherine. "Doc was right about the cinnamon rolls."

"Thank you."

"Katie, this is Jeff Hausen, a doctor from Houston. Katherine Hill."

"Known as Katie?" the man asked.

Katherine could feel Gabe's glare on her, but she smiled. "Not really. Just to people who knew me when I was a child. They don't like to let you grow up."

"Then I'm delighted to call you Katherine, because I like you all grown-up," the man said, smiling in a very friendly way.

Katherine could feel her cheeks heat up. No one had flirted with her in a long time. Except for Gabe yesterday.

"Are you on vacation?" Gabe asked suddenly, scooting his chair over by Florence. He stuck out his hand to the stranger. "Gabe Dawson."

"Sort of," Jeff said, looking askance at Doc.

"Gabe's just come back to town himself," Doc explained. "He grew up here."

"Nice town," Jeff said.

"Do you think your wife will like it?" Gabe asked, a stubborn look on his face.

Jeff looked at Katherine. "My wife is dead. So you see, Katherine, we have something in common. Doc and Florence told me about your husband. I'm sorry."

Katherine nodded slightly. The man was a little too friendly for her this morning. After all, she was—she was free, she assured herself staunchly. Absolutely free.

"How long will you be in town? Just passing through?" Gabe asked. He shot a warning look at Katherine, but she had no idea what he was trying to convey.

Florence looked at Katherine and raised her eyebrows, but Katherine shook her head. She had no idea what had gotten into Gabe, unless he was trying to determine whether the man would be here long enough to marry her. Which inspired Katherine to smile even more at the stranger.

"I haven't decided. But I'm sure I'll be here long enough to take you to dinner, Katherine. Would you come with me?"

"Katie's not interested in having dinner with you!" Gabe insisted.

Chapter Ten

Gabe couldn't believe he was acting like such a fool. He felt as awkward and unsure of himself today as he had when he was a teenager, first learning about men-women stuff.

Katie shot him a cold look before she smiled at the other man. "I'd love to have dinner with you."

"How about tonight? We could go to—" Jeff Hausen broke off and looked at Doc. "What restaurant should we go to?"

"The Last Roundup," Doc said at once. "Best place in town."

"Great. We'll go there. Is that okay with you, Katherine?"

"That would be lovely. What time?"

"What time do you finish here? I guess you'll want to go home first. I'll need to know where to pick you up."

Gabe didn't want the man going to Katie's home. He didn't want the stranger to have anything to do with Katie. But he figured he could blame himself for the turn of events more than anyone.

They were doing what he'd asked them to do.

He thought he'd made it clear yesterday, but things had gotten confused. He'd panicked when Edith had said *he* was the perfect one for Katie.

Overnight he'd changed his mind.

And he'd be encouraged if Katie had gotten mad at him for interfering in her private life. She'd always been independent. But her calm coldness was another matter.

Clearly she'd lost all interest in him.

Before Katie answered the man's question, Gabe stood. "I've got to go. Um, Florence, could I speak to you a moment?"

Katie ignored him, but Florence joined him out on the sidewalk.

"Look, yesterday, I asked you to fix Katie up, but I've changed my mind. I mean, I think she and I—I'm a little confused right now, but there's no need for you and your friends to sic half the bachelors in town on her. Or any from out of town."

Florence raised her eyebrows. Then she patted his arm. "Don't worry about it, Gabe. Things will work out." She turned to go back into the shop.

"You will call them off, won't you?" he asked, not satisfied with her answer.

Rather than tell him yes, she only smiled and went back inside. Gabe stood there, his hands on his hips, frustrated as hell.

His life was spinning out of control. In four days he'd changed his job, his home and now he was thinking about—about marrying Katie. How much change could a man deal with in such a short period of time?

Several people walked past him, staring at him as he stood in the middle of the sidewalk. Embarrassed, he spun on his heel and crossed the town square to Mac's law offices. Mac's and Alex's. And his.

The pleasure that filled him at that thought eased some of the unsettled feelings his situation with Katie caused. He hadn't been eager to go to work the past year. But now he couldn't wait to dig in.

Where to dig was the problem, he decided a few minutes later. He stood with Mac and Alex, staring at the large storage closet. "I know I'm spoiled, but I don't think I can handle this as my office," he said, looking at the other two.

"I sure couldn't," Alex agreed.

"I know, I know," Mac said. "But we've run out of space. And the beauty shop next door is wanting more space, too, so they won't be willing to give up any. What are we going to do?"

Gabe pictured in his head the square, thinking maybe they could completely move the office. Then something struck him.

"Upstairs!"

The other two stared at him. Then Mac slowly nodded. "You're right. That space has been sitting empty for almost a year. We'd have to have a stairway built, but I bet old man Hutchins would even pay for it, since it would mean more rent. I'll go call him."

"We could have a real law library," Alex added,

excitement in her voice. "And maybe even a break room, where the kids could play when I drop in for a few minutes. And—"

"Now, wait a minute. Let's take it one step at a time," Mac warned. "Let me call him."

While Mac was on the phone, Alex and Gabe walked back into her office. "When you start shopping for office furniture, you might try Melanie's consignment shop," Alex said. "Just about everything in here came from there."

"Sounds good. I like the look of it. But I'll probably need some help putting things together. I think I'm decor-challenged."

"I'll be glad to help, unless you have someone, um, special who offers."

Immediately Katie came to mind, but Gabe shook his head no. He wasn't sure she'd even speak to him again after his obnoxious behavior this morning. He'd better heed Mac's advice, taking things one step at a time.

An hour later, he was going through the rooms above the law office. Immediately, he selected the one he wanted for his office. It was a large, square corner office with big windows that looked out on the town square...and The Lemon Drop Shop.

KATIE WAS RELIEVED when Gabe disappeared. And annoyed. She'd worked hard to keep her cool when he'd behaved so badly this morning, but she wasn't sure she'd succeeded. Jeff hadn't seemed to think anything was wrong.

He was picking her up at the shop at seven. After

the lunchtime crowd had faded, she'd run home and packed up her cosmetics and an outfit, then returned to work and sent her mother home to prepare for her date. My, the Peters women were becoming real social butterflies.

Maybe she should check on Susan's social life.

Edith Hauk and Ruth Langford came into the shop, smiles on their faces. She greeted them, hoping to hide her embarrassment. The last time they'd been in, they'd discussed her and Gabe…with Gabe.

"How are you today, dear?" Edith asked after requesting a piece of carrot cake.

"Just fine. It's a lovely day."

"Yes, it is," Ruth agreed, requesting her own piece of cake and a glass of lemonade. "And it's a good thing we're looking forward to more good weather, with all the work they'll be doing to Mac's offices."

Katherine's attention was caught. "What are they doing to the law offices?"

"Well, since Gabe is joining the firm—dear, are you all right? You look like you're about to faint."

Edith chimed in, "I think you should come sit down. Mary, can you spare Katie? She's not feeling well."

Total embarrassment again, Katherine decided, as all four women, including Evelyn, hovered around her. "Please, I'm fine."

Edith led her to one of the tables and insisted she sit down.

"You hadn't heard that Gabe was staying?"

Edith asked after Katherine's two employees went back to work.

Katherine considered playacting. She'd been in the drama club in high school. But that was ten years ago. She opted for the truth. "No, I hadn't. It was a surprise."

"Well, it surprised us all, too," Ruth said, nodding. "It surprised us his mother would allow such a thing."

"Gabe's an adult," Katherine said.

Edith and Ruth rolled their eyes. "That hasn't stopped his mother yet," Edith pointed out. "I always felt sorry for Will."

"His father?" Katherine asked. "Why?"

"That poor man had to jump through hoops for his wife. She threatened to take Gabe and leave when he was little. I don't think she would have done it, but Will couldn't bear the thought. I think he finally just gave up the fight."

"I didn't know—we were so young, and didn't see much beyond our noses, you know," Katherine said, frowning as she thought back. Gabe's father had been kind, but he hadn't played much of a role in Katherine's life. Gabe's mother, on the other hand, had interfered at every turn.

"Well, I'm sure his mother is having fits…if he's told her. She hated it here in Cactus." Ruth Langford sniffed, as if to say the woman was crazy.

"And Gabe is going to actually become a partner with Mac and Alex?"

"Yes, he is. Rick Astin is going to hire them to help with his work. You know, Gabe is a contracts specialist, and a lot of Rick's business will involve contracts. They're all excited about the change.''

So she was going to have to face the fact that she could see Gabe every day for the rest of her life. Heaven and hell. He'd be just across the square. And a million miles away.

''Well, isn't that nice. I guess he's going to live at Gran's? I mean, he inherited—'' Oh, no. He couldn't remain at Gran's unless she married someone else.

And she'd vowed never to marry again unless she loved the man. And the only man she'd ever loved was Gabe Dawson. And Gabe Dawson thought the way to solve his problem was to marry her off to someone else.

Katherine felt a headache coming on.

OKAY, SO HE DIDN'T WANT steak for dinner again. But Gabe headed for The Last Roundup anyway. He heroically assured himself that he was only going to the restaurant in case Katie needed some help. After all, who knew this Jeff? He was a stranger.

Of course, he finally had to admit to himself that he was jealous as hell.

He got to the restaurant about seven, figuring that was before Katie would get there. Her shop didn't close until six and she'd need time to change out of her white-and-yellow uniform.

He'd hoped to already be seated when they arrived. Instead, they got to the door of the restaurant almost simultaneously.

"Gabe!" Katherine gasped as he held the door open for her.

"Hey, Katie, how are you?"

"Fine. You remember Jeff Hausen from—from this morning?"

He shook the man's hand. "Hello, again. From Houston, right?"

"Right." The man smiled, but he shot Gabe a speculative look, too.

Gabe couldn't blame him. He supposed his appearance did look strange.

He followed the couple, stopping as they told the hostess they were joining Samantha and Mac Gibbons. "You're eating with Mac?" he asked, surprised.

"And Samantha," Katherine added. "Oh, there they are," she exclaimed, waving to the couple in the back of the restaurant. She and Hausen started for their table.

It was the first time Gabe was able to notice Katie's outfit. He watched the seductive sway of her hips in a black knit skirt, topped by a short-sleeved, powder-blue sweater that clung in all the right places.

He swallowed hard.

Katie Peters had certainly grown up. She was all woman now, not the elfinlike fairy creature he'd fallen in love with. She'd definitely improved with age.

But more than her looks, she'd grown stronger, more determined, more sure of herself through the years. But she remained honest, always. Well, except for that one time.

"Hey, Gabe, who are you joining?" Cal asked, surprising him.

"No one. I was just looking for some dinner," he told his friend.

"Jess and I are eating here tonight. Come join us."

"I don't want to be a fifth wheel," he said, very much aware of being alone.

Cal slapped him on the shoulder. "That's okay. I've already married my girl. You're no threat to me."

Gabe laughed. "I don't think I could be called a threat to anyone," he assured his friend as he walked with him.

"Don't bet on it. You've got a few ladies in town swooning, from what I've heard."

"You shouldn't talk to your mother so much," Gabe teased. "Mabel is hell on wheels at complicating everyone's lives."

"Yeah, I heard," Cal said. But his attention was drawn to his beautiful wife, Jessica, as she met them at the back table always reserved for them and their friends.

Once they'd all greeted each other, and Gabe noted they were only a couple of tables away from Katie and her companions, he returned to Cal's comment. "You heard what?"

Cal smiled. "Mom was telling Dad about your request for them to find a man for Katie."

"Why?" Jessica asked.

"Didn't I tell you about Mrs. Dawson's will?" Cal asked his wife. At the shake of her head, he gave her the details.

"That's outrageous," Jessica said.

"It's our parents' fault. Once they succeeded, every woman in town decided she could pull off a wedding for someone," Cal pointed out.

"You could just marry Katie yourself," Jessica suggested, staring at Gabe.

He felt his cheeks redden. He swore he hadn't blushed in ten years, but these days, especially when the subject of Katie came up, he did so. "I think you may have a point."

Both Cal and Jessica stared at him.

"Are you serious?" Cal asked, his gaze shifting to Katie, two tables away with another man.

"Yeah, but I haven't said anything to her yet. I don't think she'll be very receptive to the idea."

"I thought the same thing about Jess once," Cal confessed. "I give thanks every day I was wrong." He took his wife's hand in his.

Envy shot through Gabe. He figured if he took Katie's hand in his, she'd use her other hand to slap him silly. Of course, when he'd kissed her, she hadn't slapped him, he remembered, reliving that glorious moment.

"Hey, you still with us?" Cal asked.

"Yeah."

"So when are you going to talk to Katie? And have you told her about joining Mac and Alex?"

"What's this?" Jessica asked. "Cal Baxter, you

haven't told me anything. You're going to join Mac and Alex? That's wonderful.''

Gabe nodded, smiling. He liked the feeling joining the firm gave him. ''Yeah, I'm looking forward to it.'' Then he told them about the expansion plans for the office.

''Who is Katie with tonight?'' Jessica asked, her gaze following Gabe's as he checked on Katie.

''Jeff Hausen. A friend of Doc's from Houston.'' He suddenly remembered something else. ''He's a doctor. I guess he's visiting Doc while on vacation.''

When dinner was over, Gabe watched as Jeff put an arm at Katie's trim waist to guide her outside. He clenched his fists to ward off the urge to grab that arm and shove it away from Katie. She'd chosen to go out with that man.

Tomorrow, he'd talk to Katie. Find a way to convince her to marry him, he suddenly decided. Only because that would be the most efficient way to receive his inheritance.

A temporary marriage. That was it. And it would put a stop to her seeing other men. He hadn't asked her to marry him, so she had the right to go out with another man. But once he convinced her to marry him, then she wouldn't.

Tomorrow.

THE NEXT MORNING, Katherine felt she hadn't gotten any sleep at all. After her dinner date, she'd arrived home just after her mother, Jack and Joe. They'd been joined by Susan and Paul. Conversation flew as the others caught up on Joe's life. Finally, at eleven, Katherine had insisted she had to go to bed, and the impromptu party broke up.

This morning she and her mother were in the kitchen making the carrot cakes. Mary had started the cinnamon rolls and sausage rolls as soon as she'd arrived, and now she worked the counter out front.

"Florence gave me the name of a lady she thought might want to work the morning shift," Katherine told her mother as they worked. "Ethel Moore."

"Oh, yes, I've met her. Her oldest child is in the Sunday school class I teach. Have you talked to her?"

"I thought I'd call her this morning. I'm sorry you couldn't be home to have breakfast with Joe."

"Don't worry about it. If he gets the job, he'll be around for a lot of breakfasts."

"Mom," Katherine said after a minute. "Don't be offended if Joe wants to get his own place."

Her mother looked up, staring at Katherine. "Of course not. I know money's been tight around here, but I thought you should have gotten your own place when you married. It might have saved your marriage. I've felt bad about that."

Katherine slipped two cake tins into the oven, then hugged her mother. "No, Mom, that wouldn't have made a difference. Darrell and I shouldn't have gotten married. I'm not sure I'm cut out to be a wife."

Margaret touched her daughter's cheek. "Dear,

you're perfect for marriage, as long as your husband realizes you're independent.''

Katherine laughed and moved back to pick up two more cake tins. ''Does such a man exist?''

''I hope so,'' Margaret said with a smile.

It was almost lunchtime when all the baking for the day was done. Margaret left for home with a promise to prepare a spectacular celebration dinner for Joe's return, whether he got the job or not.

Katherine had paused earlier to call Ethel Moore and asked her to come to the shop. She would be there in fifteen minutes. Katherine sent Mary on her lunch break and was tending the counter.

The doorbell jangled and she looked up. Much to her surprise, not only was Claire Dawson, Gabe's mother, standing in her shop, but she was also accompanied by a tall, modellike blonde. Katherine had seen the woman's picture once. Gran had showed her a clipping from the Dallas society page. Gabe's ex-fiancée, April.

''Good morning, may I help you?''

''Of course. We'd like two coffees,'' Mrs. Dawson said, her nose in the air. ''You work here, Katie? You do remember me, don't you?''

''Yes, Mrs. Dawson. Do you take cream or sugar?'' She looked at both of them for an answer, as if remembering Claire Dawson didn't make a bit of difference in her day.

After she served them, Claire spoke again. ''Do you have a telephone I could use? I need to call Gabe.''

Without comment, Katherine set the phone up on the counter.

"Do you have his number?"

"At Gran's—I mean, Mrs. Dawson's house? I know the old one, but—"

"No, at the law firm."

Katherine turned to the Rolodex she kept on a shelf behind the counter and gave the woman the number.

She couldn't help but hear Claire's end of the conversation. After asking for Gabe, she impatiently tapped one toe until he apparently answered.

"Gabe, darling, I'm here in Cactus. We're over at the cutest little shop, The Lemon Drop Shop. Katie works here. Can you join us?"

Apparently there was no immediate capitulation.

"But, darling, I've driven so long this morning just to visit with you.

"No, your father didn't come with me.

"Please come over here. I don't want to come there. I never cared for Mac Gibbons, or his aunt.

"Of course, dear, I understand."

When she hung up the phone, she turned to stare at Katherine, who continued to reorganize the baked goods left in the glass cases, ignoring her.

"We'll need another coffee. I believe Gabe takes it black. Isn't that right, April?" Claire cooed sweetly to the young woman.

Katherine said nothing, but she set another cup of coffee on the counter and waited to be paid.

"How long have you worked here, dear? Ever since you finished high school? Or were you working at the Dairy Queen then? It's such a long time ago, I can hardly remember. I figured you'd be a waitress at that big restaurant across the square, The Last Roundup. I heard you were a very good waitress.''

Katherine said nothing. She knew the woman wasn't being friendly. She was getting in as many jabs as possible while smiling.

The doorbell jangled again, and Gabe entered.

''Darling,'' Claire exclaimed, hugging him. ''I'm so glad you could spare the time. I brought you a surprise!'' she said with the flare of a magician's assistant. ''Your fiancée, April!''

Chapter Eleven

Gabe shot a quick glance at Katie, only to see her disappear through the kitchen door. He turned back to scowl at his mother. "We all know that April is no longer my fiancée, Mom."

"Nonsense, darling, she's forgiven you. There's no need to crawl back to Cactus to lick your wounds." She took his arm and tried to tug him over to the table where the blonde waited.

"Licking my wounds is a rather inappropriate expression. Had there been wounds that severe, I would have bled to death seven years ago. Fortunately, neither of us suffered from our breakup, right, April?"

"I thought you'd change your mind again, Gabe. I understood you just needed a little space," April assured him with a bland smile.

"And you've been patient for seven years?" he returned, scorn in his voice. "What happened to the millionaire you had on a string? At least that's what I heard."

April stirred in her chair and looked away. "He wasn't right for me."

"Here's your coffee, Gabe," his mother interrupted, handing him a cup. "Little Katie Peters was serving us. Too bad she's never accomplished anything with her life. But then, there aren't many opportunities for the uneducated in a small town."

"Stop being rude, Mother," he growled.

"Why, darling, don't be silly. I was feeling sorry for her, not criticizing her. It's hard when you come from a big family. So—so *bourgeois*," she finished with a delicate shudder.

A cool voice announced Katherine's return. "Isn't it, though. Do you need refills?"

"Why, no, dear, but thank you for asking. I'm afraid your coffee doesn't quite compare to Starbucks. They make the most divine—"

"Mother! I think you'd better leave." Gabe had had enough of his mother's condescending patter.

"Of course, darling, as soon as you agree to come with us." She leaned closer to Gabe. "You know, your father misses you desperately. I'm really getting worried about him."

Gabe had spoken to his father about an hour ago. Will had listed his condo with a Realtor and arranged for movers to pack and ship his belongings. He'd also been to Gabe's office to make similar arrangements. And he'd sounded more cheerful than he had in years.

"Then you should be home with him," he returned calmly.

"Well, really, dear, I lead a busy life. I can't baby-sit a grown man."

"Without his money, I suspect your life would be a lot less busy. You'd have to get a job. Ever think of that, Mom?"

"Darling Gabe, this town has affected your brain. Come along, and we'll go pack your things."

Gabe looked at Katie, standing behind the counter, pretending not to listen to their conversation. "I'm staying right here, Mom. I'm going to work with Mac and Alex, I'm going to live in Gran's house—and I'm going to be happy."

He'd almost announced to his mother that he was going to marry Katie, but good sense had stopped him. She'd never forgive him—or marry him—for any reason if he'd made that mistake.

Instead of getting upset, Claire looked at April. "I told you this might take some time. I suppose we'll just have to dig in our heels." Then she turned back to Gabe. "Which bedrooms shall we take? Or do you want April to share yours?"

"*Share?*" Gabe bellowed.

"Well, darling, I am a modern woman. I know you and April have been, shall we say, intimate? I understand a virile man's needs."

He clenched his teeth. "If you and April insist on staying, I'll make you a reservation at the bed-and-breakfast on the square."

"No, dear, I want to stay with you. There are three bedrooms," she said with a sigh, "so until you get straightened out, I guess we can manage."

She stood and held out a hand. "The keys, please, dear."

Gabe closed his eyes. His immediate response was to tell her to sleep on the street. He was not going to be manipulated by his mother ever again. But she *was* his mother. He couldn't humiliate her that way. And it wasn't as if he couldn't resist April.

"The back door's not locked."

Claire rolled her eyes, then nodded. "We'll fix a lovely dinner and expect you home by six." Then, with a condescending nod to Katie, she motioned for April to follow her and left the shop.

Once the two women had departed, Gabe turned to face Katie, embarrassed by his mother's behavior. "Katie—"

"I'm back," Mary sang out. "Ready for a break?" she asked as she came through the kitchen door.

Gabe knew his face reflected his distaste for her interruption, but—

The bell over the door jangled as someone entered. "Mrs. Hill?" a soft voice called.

"If you'll excuse me, Gabe?" Katie said, no emotion on her face.

As if he had a choice. "We'll talk later," he growled and stalked out of the shop, too.

ETHEL MOORE WAS PERFECT for the job. A quiet, pleasant woman, she loved to cook and got along well with both Evelyn and Mary. Katherine hired her on the spot, glad something was going well. She agreed to start the next morning.

Katherine spent all afternoon doing book work, now that both Mary and Evelyn were working the counter. It helped keep her mind off Gabe and his mother. And April.

And the fact that the two women were going to be staying in Gran's house. With all that had happened lately, Katherine understood some of the comments Gran had made to her toward the end. And why she'd left her estate to Gabe, rather than her own son.

It was another example of a marriage gone bad. Katherine guessed Gabe's father was miserable. As she had been. Which only underlined her determination not to remarry except for the right reason.

Which brought her back to Gabe's problem.

She redoubled her efforts to do the books.

"HE WAS GREAT!" Joe was exclaiming when Katherine came through the back door.

"Who was great?" she asked, taking in the pleased expressions around the room. Maybe they would have something to celebrate after all.

"Mr. Astin. He hired me, Katie! And I don't have to wait until fall. I'm going to get in on the ground floor. He's putting the company together at his office at the ranch, where we did the interview. There'll be a start-up team of five of us."

"That's wonderful, Joe," Katherine said, swooping down on him to give him a sisterly hug. "I bet Mom's thrilled."

"Yeah," he said, a huge grin on his face.

"Of course I am, but I knew all along Rick would hire him. He's a very smart boy." Margaret looked at Jack for confirmation and he, of course, nodded.

"But last night—" Susan began, but Paul hugged her, then whispered something in her ear. Hopefully something that would keep Susan from reminding her mother of her fears from the night before.

"Well, are you ready to eat, Katie? I've got a great meal all prepared for our celebration," Margaret said. "I only wish Diane and Raine could be here. But we'll call them after dinner and tell them the good news."

Katherine took her belongings to her bedroom, changed out of her yellow-and-white uniform into jeans and washed up before returning to the big kitchen. Just as she did so, a vehicle pulled into their driveway.

"Hey, it's Gabe," Paul exclaimed, and hurried to the back door.

"Gabe Dawson?" Joe inquired. "Is he back in town?" His gaze shot to Katherine, who strived to keep her cheeks from turning red.

"Yes, he's settling his grandmother's estate, I believe," Jack said.

"I heard he's staying," Margaret said.

Paul came back in alone. "Gabe wants to talk to you," he said, looking at Katherine. "Alone," he added as everyone stared at her.

"Well, for land's sake, Katie, invite him to

dinner. He's probably starved since it's six-thirty already,'' Margaret said. ''Never mind, I will.'' And she hurried outside.

Katherine didn't think Gabe would accept. After all, if he hadn't eaten already, she knew he had a home-cooked meal awaiting him at Gran's house.

Margaret came back in, with Gabe on her heels. ''I told him we're celebrating. You can talk to him after dinner, Katie.'' Margaret was beaming, pleased that more people would be praising Joe.

Katherine looked at their new guest. ''I thought you already had dinner plans?''

Gabe replied, ''Nope.'' No elaboration.

Okay, so he wasn't cooperating with his mother…yet. But Katherine knew he loved his father. She suspected Mrs. Dawson would get her way eventually.

Over dinner, Joe repeated every aspect of his successful interview for Gabe's benefit. Gabe, in turn, told everyone about his joining Alex and Mac, about working on contracts already for Rick's new business.

Katherine managed to slip in the fact that she'd hired Ethel Moore to work mornings for her, so her mother wouldn't have to abandon her family before dawn each day.

''I feel badly about that,'' Margaret said, frowning. ''I thought maybe you could use the extra money to get your own place.''

Gabe stiffened. ''You're moving out?''

''I never said that, Mom,'' Katherine said, directing her gaze to her mother.

"I know, but I've thought about it. You warned me about Joe wanting his own place. I bet you only thought of that because *you* want your own place."

Katherine fought to keep a calm smile on her face. "I was protecting Paul's bedroom. I have designs on it once he goes to college."

"Hey! I'm not leaving forever!" the boy protested.

Everyone laughed and conversation became general again, relieving Katherine.

She didn't want to discuss anything about her family in front of Gabe. His mother's words today still stung. Even though she didn't believe Gabe felt like his mother, they'd hurt.

After Margaret served chocolate pie, Gabe looked directly at Katherine. "Can we go for a ride?"

"It's been a long day, Gabe. Maybe another time?" When hell froze over. He could go spend time with April instead.

"I have some things I need to talk to you about, Katie, and they won't wait. If you want your family—"

Her anger flared. "Don't try to manipulate me, Gabe Dawson! You may have learned from the best, but I'm not going to cooperate."

Gabe smiled, obviously recognizing her reference to his mother. "I need to apologize for today."

"No! It doesn't matter," she said hurriedly, and jumped up to carry dirty dishes to the sink.

"What happened today?" Joe asked.

"Nothing!" Katherine said, her voice louder than she'd intended.

"My mother came to town. She managed to offend half the population of Cactus inside of an hour, Katie included."

She put down the dishes and whirled around. "Gabe, there's no need to discuss this any further."

"I think there is. But we have other topics to consider, too. That's why I asked you to go for a ride." He stared at her, his brown eyes gleaming. Was he laughing at her?

"Not tonight."

"The other thing I wanted to discuss was Gran's will," Gabe said calmly, as if she'd asked him a question.

She weighed the pros and cons of trying to stall the blasted man, or letting him have his private discussion. She hated to give in, but she didn't want her family in on this discussion. "Fine!" she snapped. "We'll talk outside."

GABE THANKED MARGARET for the dinner, congratulated Joe again and excused himself. He'd decided on his approach to Katie, but he hadn't wanted to try it in front of an audience.

Katie was standing like a soldier on guard on the back porch, her arms rigid at her side. She glared at him and said nothing.

"Sure you don't want to go for a ride?" he tried again.

"No!"

"Okay. We'll start with my mother...and April.

They were rude this morning with no reason. My mother thought she was being clever with her smart-ass remarks.''

"I told you it didn't matter.''

"But it does, Katie,'' he insisted. "You've worked harder than my mother ever has. And you've supported your family when it wasn't your job. You own your own business. Everyone loves you.'' He smiled. "My mother can't claim any of those accomplishments, especially the last one.''

She crossed her arms over her chest and turned away from him. "It doesn't matter,'' she repeated.

He moved closer and took her shoulders in his hands. Unfortunately, she jerked away from him and moved as far from him as she could and still be on the porch.

Which only confirmed he'd chosen the correct approach.

"We need to talk about Gran's will,'' he finally said.

"There's nothing to talk about. You said there was nothing to do.'' She kept her back to him.

"You know that's not true. There are two options. The easiest one is for you to marry someone else.'' He prayed he was handling this situation right. He'd die if she selected that option.

"Easiest for whom?'' she snapped. "Not me! I've been in a loveless marriage. I won't do that.''

Relief swept through him.

"Well, there's another option.''

She turned to stare at him. "What? Are you

going to try to prove Gran was incompetent? I don't think—"

"No. But you haven't forgotten you said you'd help me, have you?"

Her gaze grew cautious. "No, I haven't forgotten. And I will if I can."

"It's pretty simple. Gran's will said we had to marry, but it doesn't say how long we have to be married. If we married for a few months, a pretend marriage," he hurriedly added, as her eyes widened in shock, "then we could have it annulled after the year is up."

"Wouldn't that be illegal? I told you I wouldn't do anything illegal."

He took a step closer to her, knowing she couldn't retreat any farther without getting off the porch. "It would be a real marriage. The marriage vows don't say we have to sleep together. We can share Gran's house—platonically—for a few months. There are three bedrooms. You can have the third one to do whatever you intended to do with Paul's."

"Resorting to bribery?" she asked, her beautiful lips quirking at the corners.

He smiled in return, glad to see some of her anger disappear.

"I don't have a problem with bribery. I'm even willing to offer a bonus. After all, you'll be losing quite a bit of money if you marry me." He knew he'd made another mistake as her features tightened again.

"I don't want Gran's money. I never—I didn't

know she was going to do that. It all belongs to you. But it feels like we're—I don't want to do the wrong thing.''

He shrugged his shoulders, hoping to regain lost ground. ''It's the only thing I can think of. And I'd suggest you ask Mac, but if we tell him we're trying to get out of the requirements of the will, I'm not sure our plan would work.''

She covered her face with her hands. Then she took her hands down and stared at him. ''I need some time to think.''

''Of course. I understand. I'd appreciate your helping me out, but if you decide you can't, well, I'll understand that, too.'' He figured he'd better get out of there before he cradled her against him, hoping to remove that worried look from her face.

And hoping to feel her body against his one more time.

He backed off the porch. ''Sorry I manipulated you, Katie. I hate it when my mother does that, but I had to speak to you alone.''

She nodded but said nothing.

''Well—'' he cleared his throat ''—uh, let me know when you make up your mind. Or, if you have any questions.''

''What about April? Are you going to marry her after we—after our marriage is annulled?''

He gave a sardonic laugh. ''In my mother's dreams. But no other way. No, I don't have any plans for that.''

''But they're at your house.''

''Yeah. Hopefully, when I didn't show up for

dinner, they got disgusted and headed for Dallas.'' He knew he was being too much of an optimist. But a guy could hope.

''I'll let you know as soon as I can,'' she assured him, that worried look returning to her face.

He stepped back up on the porch and risked brushing his lips against hers. ''Stop worrying. Everything will work out.''

Then he hurried to his car before she could reject him outright.

Driving to Gran's house, he reviewed his plan again. He had figured the one thing that Katie always did was help someone in trouble. If she responded to his plea and married him, he'd have a lot of time to convince her their marriage could work out.

But he wouldn't use manipulation. If she didn't believe that, then he'd keep his hands to himself. He would. But it'd be a living hell.

An appropriate thought, he acknowledged as he pulled into Gran's driveway. His mother's Mercedes was parked by the back door.

Groaning, he parked his car beside it, making a mental note to himself to trade in his Mercedes as soon as possible. It had been another choice his mother had encouraged.

When he entered the back door, his mother was standing in the kitchen, her arms crossed and indignation on her face.

''Where have you been? Dinner is cold!''

April was nowhere in sight.

"Then you should've eaten it when it was hot," he said calmly.

Claire stared at him in shock. "How dare you speak to me like that!"

"What did I say that was so terrible?"

"I slaved over a hot stove for you!" she exclaimed, glaring at him.

He looked at the table. "Number one, Mom, you *told* me to be home at six for dinner. You didn't ask me. Number two, that food looks remarkably like food from The Last Roundup, which means you lied about cooking it."

"We didn't have time to cook. We had to pack your belongings, Gabe, darling, so we could get out of this forsaken place first thing in the morning."

He shook his head. "The only place I'm going in the morning is to work in downtown Cactus."

"Downtown! Ha! You're doing no such thing. I've managed to get your job back for you, but you've got to call your boss and tell him it's what you want. The man wouldn't take my word for it," Claire grumbled.

"Mom, I'm not going back. I don't want that job. I'm staying here."

"I won't stand for it!" she shrieked.

April appeared in the doorway, dressed in a silk negligee. "Your way isn't working, Claire. I think it's time I took over." She crossed to Gabe's side and ran one hand up his chest. "Darling, let's discuss everything in a more comfortable place." She grabbed his tie and tried to pull him toward the bedrooms.

"*We* have nothing to discuss," he said coolly, refusing to budge.

His mother began to shriek again.

Until a quiet voice from the door stopped her.

"That's enough, Claire."

Chapter Twelve

Katherine met her new employee and Mary at the shop at six the next morning. They worked well together as a team. By noon, things had slowed down and Katherine had time to think.

Too much time.

She'd scarcely slept the night before, thinking about Gabe's proposal. She'd once dreamed of hearing him propose marriage. Then it had happened. Wrong time. Now it had happened again. But it wasn't real.

They never seemed to get it right.

Nevertheless, she'd promised to help him. She believed it would be wrong, not what Gran wanted, for Gabe to lose his inheritance.

But would they be doing something wrong to marry without intending to fulfill their marriage vows?

Finally she picked up the phone and called Alex Langford at home.

"Alex, I know it's Saturday, but I have a problem, a big problem. Could you meet me in town for an hour?''

''Sure, I can, Katie. I can be at the office in half an hour.''

''Uh, not the office,'' Katherine hurriedly said. ''I think Gabe is working today.''

''What's the matter with that man? Working on a Saturday?'' Alex teased. ''He'll ruin our laid-back reputation.''

Much to Katherine's relief, she didn't ask why Katherine wanted to avoid Gabe.

''We could have a late lunch at The Last Roundup, if that's okay,'' Alex suggested.

''That would be wonderful,'' Katherine agreed. ''I'll meet you there at one o'clock.''

Leaving her shop in Mary and Evelyn's hands, she hurried home and changed out of her uniform. She didn't want to wear it to lunch.

Alex was already seated in a booth and waved at Katherine when she came in. She hurried over, after scanning the room. She didn't want Gabe to see them.

''Are we doing something secretive?'' Alex asked, leaning forward and whispering.

''Sort of.''

''Great. I love it!'' Alex returned with a big grin.

They placed their orders, then Alex looked at her expectantly.

''Do you remember our discussion about Mrs. Dawson's will?'' Katherine began.

Alex nodded.

''Whatever I say to you is protected by lawyer-client privilege, isn't it?'' Katherine wanted to be sure of that before she continued.

Alex nodded again.

''Gabe has asked me to marry him for a few months, until the will issue is resolved. Then we'll annul the marriage.'' She kept her gaze on Alex. ''Is that illegal?''

Alex's eyebrows climbed. ''Illegal? Hmm.'' She stared across the restaurant, considering her words. ''No, I don't think so. After all, the will doesn't mention consummation, only marriage.''

''But—''

''I'll admit, it's not in the spirit of the will, but you're only held to the wording of it.''

''But if Mac knew, could he invalidate our— could he stop Gabe from inheriting?''

''No. But I don't think you should tell anyone, Katie. The less people who know, the better off you'll be.''

''Why, if we're not doing anything wrong?''

''Because it's probable the charity scheduled to receive the other half of Mrs. Dawson's estate would sue…and quite possibly win.''

''I never thought of that!'' Katherine said with a gasp.

''That's why you pay me the big bucks,'' Alex teased. ''Mac had to notify them of their contingency inheritance and they asked that he keep them informed of events.''

Katherine frowned, feeling guilty that a charity would be denied funds because of her actions. But she still believed Gabe deserved his inheritance. In fact, she believed Gran wanted it that way.

"Besides, it would be too hard on a man's ego to admit that a beautiful woman was marrying him but he wouldn't be able to sleep with her," Alex added.

Katherine's face flamed. "Gabe doesn't want— he's not interested in—"

Alex laughed. "Oh, Katie, all men are interested in that. Fortunately, the good ones care about other things, too, but they're all interested in sex."

"I'll vote for that," Tuck Langford said, appearing at their table and scooting his wife over. After he'd sat down, he said, "Mind if I join you?"

"It's a little late to ask, isn't it? And where is the baby? I left you to baby-sit," Alex pointed out.

"That's what grandmothers are for," Tuck assured her with a grin.

Alex looked at Katherine. "He's got his mother convinced the baby will come to irreparable harm if Tuck is left in charge."

Katherine grinned, but inside she ached with jealousy. She wanted her own baby, her own family, her...own love. Instead, it appeared she was going to have a sham.

"Do you two ladies need to discuss any more business?" Tuck asked, serious for the first time.

"No," Katherine assured him. "I think we've covered everything, haven't we?" She looked at Alex.

"Yes, we have. Unless you have any more questions."

"No, I—"

"Mind if I join you?" a deep voice asked.

Katherine knew who it was, of course. But, at least with Tuck there, maybe Gabe wouldn't suspect her of telling Alex the truth. She scooted over to make room for Gabe.

"Hey, buddy, how's it going?" Tuck asked, greeting his old friend. "Are those horses working out? Spence was pleased to find a good home for that little filly. Have you ridden her yet, Katie?"

"Ridden a filly? What filly?"

Gabe stirred, then cleared his throat. "I bought a couple of horses from Spence. I thought maybe we'd go for a ride sometime...like we used to."

Katherine could feel her cheeks heating up, just thinking about their activities on those rides. "No, I haven't gone riding," she told Tuck, keeping her gaze away from Gabe.

"There hasn't been time. I just bought them a couple of days ago," Gabe added. "Things are happening so fast in my life, I think I'm going crazy."

"You made the right decision to stay, though," Tuck assured him. "Life here is a lot sweeter than in those big cities."

Alex jabbed her husband in his ribs. "How would you know? You've never lived in a big city."

"Nope. I'm too smart for that."

"So you're saying I'm dumb?" Gabe asked, in mock indignation.

Tuck shook his head, but he was grinning.

"Nope, but you had some, uh, influences that helped you make your decision."

Gabe nodded. "Speaking of which, my mother arrived in town yesterday."

Katherine kept her head down, but the other two looked at each other and then Gabe.

"Everyone knows that," Tuck said.

"Yeah. She's not an easy person," Gabe said. "I think she offended half the population."

Tuck leaned toward Gabe. "I wouldn't bring her in here to eat, either. She insisted on inspecting the kitchen before she'd order something to go. Made a *big* impression."

Gabe groaned. "Now I guess I owe Jess an apology."

"Nah. We all know you're not like that," Tuck assured him.

"I'm so sorry I didn't get to meet this legend," Alex said, grinning. "Did you talk to her?" she asked, looking at Katherine.

She nodded and didn't say anything.

Gabe laid his arm on the back of the booth, almost touching Katherine. She hadn't expected such friendliness.

"She saved her best for Katie. She was always afraid Katie would keep me from 'reaching my potential.'"

Katherine tried to relax, but she couldn't. "She was right," she muttered, staring at her hands clasped on the table. "If I'd accepted your proposal, you wouldn't have gone to law school."

"I could have gone to law school at Tech," he

said, putting his other hand over hers. "Or I could have found something else to do. And still been happy."

"But you love being a lawyer!" Katherine exclaimed.

"Yeah, but—"

"Can't change the past," Tuck reminded them. "Time to move on, boys and girls. It's not too late, you know. Cactus is a great place for weddings."

His wife elbowed him again.

Gabe opened his mouth and Katherine was afraid of what he might say. She changed the subject. "Speaking of weddings, I think my mother and Jack are going to finally set a date."

WHEN LUNCH WAS OVER, the foursome strolled back outside, reveling in the beautiful weather. Everything was green and new and the sun shone brightly.

"Today might be a good day to try out those horses, Katie," Gabe suggested.

"I don't think your mother would approve."

"Doesn't much matter. She's left town."

"I thought she was going to stay until you moved back with her?"

"Whoa! That's one determined woman," Tuck commented.

"Yeah, but my dad arrived and routed her."

Alex looked at first Tuck and then Katie. "Why are you both looking so surprised?"

It was Gabe who answered. "Because my father

has always caved in to Mom's demands. This time he didn't.''

"Why the change?" Tuck asked.

"He's divorcing her."

The other three gasped, shocked by his words.

Gabe explained. "She always threatened to leave him and take me with her. Dad couldn't stomach that thought. After a while, giving in to her became a habit. I reminded him that she couldn't take me away any longer. He's been very unhappy."

"Maybe if they tried counseling..." Katherine began.

"It won't help. It's been a long time coming," Gabe said, staring at her.

She raised her blue eyes and returned his look, then dropped her gaze and shook her head.

"Yeah." He agreed with everything he'd seen in those eyes, the sadness of a marriage that didn't work, the pain involved. "So, how about a ride?"

Before Katherine could answer, Tuck intervened. "Hey, come out to the ranch. The other guys are coming about two and doing some roping, some cutting. We don't do much of the hard stuff, like bulls or broncos, 'cause our wives don't like it," he added, pretending to scowl at Alex, "but we have a lot of fun."

"I don't have a trailer to haul my horses over there," Gabe admitted, disappointed because he'd enjoy the afternoon. It had been a long time since he'd swung a rope.

"I've got plenty of horses. Is your dad still in

town? Invite him to come, too. Then we'll all have dinner together. It'll be fun.''

"How about it, Katie?" he asked, unwilling to commit himself without her.

"You don't need me. I've got—"

"Nope. If you don't go, I'm not going."

"Isn't that called cutting off your nose to spite your face?" she asked, raising her eyebrows.

The urge to kiss her soft lips was almost more than he could stand, but he couldn't afford to scare her off. "Nope, it's good thinking. I—"

"Come on, Katie," Alex urged. "It's a lot of fun. It's a potluck dinner. The ladies don't usually come over until about four. Everyone brings their kids. You can play with all the babies and catch up on the gossip."

"It sounds like fun. And I'd have time to finish my paperwork. But what shall I bring?"

"First-timers don't have to bring anything," Alex assured her.

Katie smiled. "I'll bring some dessert."

Tuck grinned. "That's what I was hopin'!"

Alex scolded her husband, then they said their goodbyes and crossed the square to the law offices.

Gabe took Katie's hand. "You're sure you'll come? I can come back and pick you up so you won't have to—"

"I'm not incapable of driving, Gabe. And I told Alex I'd come."

He pulled her hand to his chest, pressing it over his heartbeat. "Who cares about Alex? *I* want to know you're coming."

Her teeth sank into her bottom lip and he thought he'd die from desire. "I'll be there," she said softly.

Okay, so he'd told himself not to pressure her, but he had to taste those lips. He had to remember the sweetness that her lips brought to him. He had to...

When he lifted his head, she was frowning, but she didn't protest.

"I'll see you then," he whispered, and turned away before she could change her mind.

"Gabe?" she called, stopping him in his tracks.

Was she going to take her acceptance back? Damn, he hoped not. Slowly he turned to face her. "Yeah?"

"Be careful."

Relief filled him and a grin spread across his face. "Oh, I am, Katie, I am." Then he realized what he'd said. "I mean, I will. I'll be careful."

WHEN KATHERINE PARKED her car at Tuck and Alex's ranch, she was relieved to see it wasn't a small gathering. She could avoid any private moments with Gabe.

Private? The man had kissed her on the town square. She needed to avoid him period.

How are you going to do that after you marry him?

That question had been bothering her all day. She'd already decided she had no choice but to marry Gabe...in name only. In theory, she believed it was the right decision. But the thought of living in the same house with him, sharing his meals, his life, sent panic through her veins. If she was within ten feet of the man, she wanted to touch him.

Poor Darrell, with all his attempts, had never stirred even a tenth of the desire Gabe could arouse with a look.

"Katie? Come on in!" Alex called from the front door.

Katherine realized she'd been sitting in her car, staring into space for several minutes. With a wave, she grabbed the large Pyrex dish on the seat beside her and headed for the house.

"What did you bring?" Alex asked, her gaze fastened on the dish.

"It's a new recipe I'm trying out. It's kind of a peach cobbler but it has cream cheese in it. I thought I'd use everyone as guinea pigs."

Will Dawson appeared behind Alex. "Let me be the first to volunteer. How are you, Katie?"

"Fine, thank you, Mr. Dawson. Welcome back to Cactus."

"Thanks, and make it Will."

Katie wondered just how much Gabe's father knew about their situation. Not that it mattered. She wasn't going to say anything. She moved into the kitchen and discovered it filled with women from Cactus.

Alex began introducing her to some newcomers. Megan Astin, Rick's wife, was far advanced in her pregnancy. Katie urged her not to stand when they were introduced.

She laughed. "Thanks. It's not like I can pop up and down easily."

"Does your husband play cowboy, too?" Katherine asked, frowning. "I thought he was a computer expert."

"Yes, but he was raised on a farm, and we have our own ranch, now. It's just next door."

Jessica, Cal's wife, grinned. "They never outgrow the urge to be a cowboy. Did I hear you say you've brought a new dessert?" Since she used Katherine's carrot cakes in her restaurant, it pleased Katherine that she seemed interested.

"Yes. It's a peach cobbler, but the recipe includes cream cheese and some other things. It's a little lighter than the carrot cake."

"I can't wait. Can we start with dessert, Alex?" Jessica asked with a laugh.

Though several people seconded the idea, Alex shook her head no. "Our cowboys would never forgive us. Katie, do you want to see the boys at play, or do you want to check out the babies? We've been outside, but it's warming up in the afternoons these days, and we got hot."

"I'd like to play with the babies, but maybe later. I've heard about these rodeos you've been having, but I've never seen one, so I'll go outside for a little while." She didn't want to admit that she was anxious to be sure Gabe was all right. He was used to tending legal files, not cows.

Melanie Hauk, Spence's wife and owner of the consignment shop on the square, waved at Katie. "Follow me. I promised Spence I'd come back out after I checked on our son. He's still down for his nap.''

"Are you sure, Melanie? I can go by myself,'' Katherine assured her. They had become friends at the Chamber of Commerce meetings. Not too many businesses were run by women, so she, Katherine and Jessica had grown close.

As she followed Melanie, Jessica, Alex and Samantha, Mac's wife, joined them.

"I'm glad Megan's not coming out. How much longer does she have?'' Jessica asked Samantha.

"A few weeks yet, but she needs to stay off her feet when she has the chance.'' Samantha looked at Katherine. "I hear your mom is about to get married. I think that's great.''

"I may need to call you,'' Katherine said, smiling. "You've had experience with a parent marrying. At least,'' she began when she remembered Florence wasn't Samantha's mother. "Kind of. Florence isn't —''

"Yes, she is, in every sense of the word,'' Samantha assured her. "I know all about arranging weddings. We all have a lot of experience doing that,'' she added with a grin.

"Yeah, but I don't think you want a wedding like Sam and Mac's,'' Alex said. "We all three went into labor at the altar.''

Katherine joined the laughter. "I don't think that's possible, since the only pregnant person I know is Megan Astin, and I just met her. Oh, and you. But you're not far enough along to surprise us.''

"Good," Alex said.

"So, when are you going to test the romantic waters again?" Jessica asked. "Since Gabe came back to town, it seems to me he's shown a lot of interest in you."

Katherine didn't know where to look. Whatever she said would be wrong. She didn't want to say his interest was in his inheritance. She didn't want to say they were marrying, because she hadn't talked to him, and he should be the first to know her decision. She didn't want to say she was crazy about the man. She definitely didn't want to say that.

That was a secret she'd have to keep from everyone.

Even herself, if she could.

Alex came to her rescue. "Jess, you sound as bad as our mothers-in-law. Katie is concentrating on her career."

"A very successful career," Melanie added in support.

"We'll see how successful when you taste my cobbler," Katherine said, hoping to tease Jessica away from her earlier question.

She knew she'd been successful when Jessica's eyes flashed in her direction. "I can't wait. I had no idea you were experimenting with other recipes."

Then, just as Katherine was breathing a sigh of relief, she added, "Of course, you can have a career and babies at the same time. The four of us are prime examples, you know."

"I think you need a husband before you start with the babies," Katherine said, trying to keep her smile in place.

Hard, warm arms slid around her and a deep voice said, "Hey, I'll volunteer."

Chapter Thirteen

Gabe felt Katie's body stiffen, but he didn't back off. It felt too good to hold her again.

"Gabe!" she protested, and shoved against his arms.

Jessica grinned. "I always say you can't go wrong with a good volunteer."

"Now all we have to do is convince Katie," Gabe said, grinning in return.

"I know some ladies who might be able to help," Jessica told him. "They're experts on this matchmaking thing."

"No!" Gabe protested too loudly. "I mean, I, uh, I don't need any help."

This time Katie shoved hard enough to force him to release her...unless he wanted everyone to know she didn't want to be in his arms. "He's already consulted them," she said.

"Really?" Jessica said, her eyes widening.

"But he wasn't volunteering himself," Katie continued, as if Jessica hadn't spoken. "He was volunteering any male within a hundred-mile radius, as long as it *wasn't* him.''

Gabe swallowed his groan. She would have to announce his mistake to the world. ''Uh, I changed my mind.''

''I'll say,'' Alex agreed.

''Hey!'' Spence called from the corral. ''Mel, are you coming?''

Melanie smiled. ''Sorry, my man gets impatient.'' She left the circle of friends and hurried to Spence's side.

Gabe snatched Katie's hand, afraid she'd run away from him. He wished he had the right to claim her time, like Spence had with his woman. ''Did you come out to watch? Spence is about to demonstrate his roping ability.''

''Yes, I wanted to see it. Have you been roping?''

Was there a spark of concern in her blue eyes? He hoped so. With a rueful grin, he admitted, ''Yeah. But I'm kind of rusty.''

Cal, having come to meet Jessica, laughed behind them. ''Rusty? That's an understatement. He's going to have to practice a lot before roundup.''

''Roundup?'' Katie asked in surprise. ''But he's a lawyer, Cal. He won't—''

''Mac always shuts down the office during roundup, Katie. Gabe won't want to miss it, either. Though we may have to put him in charge of the chuck wagon if he doesn't improve,'' Cal added with a laugh.

Katie squeezed his hand, as if for comfort, and

Gabe felt warm all over. He didn't mind Cal's teasing. He hadn't been that bad. But he loved the idea of Katie worrying that his feelings might be hurt.

"Now that I'm back in Cactus, I'll have time to practice. Pretty soon, I'll be able to beat your sorry butt, Cal Baxter. You're too busy chasing bad guys."

Cal laughed. "Yeah, we have so many of them in Cactus."

A shout from the house had everyone turning in that direction in time to see Doc and Jeff Hausen step out of the house.

"What's *he* doing here?" Gabe asked with a frown. He didn't want anyone but married men around Katie.

When Katie actually waved to the man, he dropped her hand and wrapped an arm around her shoulders. She looked up at him in surprise.

"I was afraid you might be cold," he muttered.

"Gabe, it's almost eighty this afternoon," she informed him.

"Uh-huh. Come on, let me introduce you to the horse I've been riding. He's a good one." He pulled her toward the corral. And away from Jeff Hausen.

A couple of hours later, when he'd exhausted every trick he knew to keep Katie to himself, everyone went inside to eat. Katie offered to get their drinks if he'd fill their plates. He had no objection because that meant she intended to eat with him.

His father found a chair on his other side.

"You doing all right, Dad?" he asked softly.

"Better than I have in a long time," Will said

with a smile. "I've been playing forty-two with some old friends. It felt good."

Gabe smiled, glad his father wasn't feeling left out.

"Will, do you want me to get you some iced tea, too?" Katie asked as she set the glasses down on the table.

"Thank you, Katie. That would be nice." As Katie walked away, he added, "She's a beautiful woman, inside and out."

"Yeah. I'm trying to convince her to marry me."

"Good for you." Though he smiled, Gabe noted concern in his gaze.

"You don't approve?"

"Of course I do. Though I hope you're marrying her for the right reasons and not to get back at your mother."

"I've had the right reasons about Katie for ten years. I'm just finally letting them surface."

"Okay. Then it looks like I'll need to find somewhere else to live."

"No! I didn't mean—"

"Don't worry about it, boy. There are lots of places for me to light. It doesn't have to be in your back pocket."

Katie returned with another glass of tea and gave it to Will.

"Thanks, Katie." Then he looked over Katie's shoulder. "Hello, I don't think I've met you."

Gabe's head jerked up to find Jeff Hausen standing behind Katie. "Uh, this is Jeff Hausen, Dad. Jeff, my father, Will Dawson."

The two men shook hands just as Florence and George Greenfield sat down across from them.

Doc Greenfield said, "I heard you're thinking of moving back here, like your son, Will. We all sure would like that."

Gabe didn't pay much attention to the general conversation. Jeff was talking to Katie, and Gabe was much more interested in what the man was saying. Until Doc dropped his bombshell.

"No, I'm going to completely retire, except for emergencies and filling in."

It was as if a bomb had gone off. Everyone in the room stopped their noisy conversations and turned in their direction. Then a burst of questions demolished the silence.

Doc raised both hands. "Now, folks, I'd intended to make the announcement tomorrow. But I guess I jumped the gun. Jeff has agreed to come to Cactus as our full-time doctor, while Samantha continues to work part-time."

Ed Baxter, one of Doc's old-time friends, asked, "But Doc, what are you going to do? You're not old enough to sit in a rocker all day."

"You're right. I'm going to become County Medical Examiner. They've decided we're populated enough to need one instead of sending to Lubbock every time a body shows up."

There was a round of applause, but Gabe didn't join in. The most significant part of Doc's speech was when he said Jeff Hausen would be moving to Cactus permanently.

And the man was flirting with Katie.

Gabe slid an arm around Katie and leaned toward Jeff.

"When are you moving to Cactus? I imagine it will take a while to make the transfer."

"Not really. I'm planning on being moved in in a couple of weeks. I found a place to live this afternoon."

"But it will be major shock, coming from a big town like Houston, to Cactus," Gabe insisted.

"You just moved from Dallas, and you look to be doing pretty well," the doctor pointed out with a grin. Which found an answering smile from Katie.

"But I grew up here. It's different. Besides, I have friends here, like Katie." He tightened his hold on her shoulder.

Jeff lifted a brow. "I'm hoping I can count on Katherine as a friend, also."

Gabe wanted to shout that Katie was his, and Jeff couldn't have her, but he knew that wouldn't win him any brownie points with Katie. So he had two weeks to make sure she was his before the good doctor came back to town.

KATHERINE WAS FLATTERED by the doctor's attention, but Gabe's obvious jealousy was even more pleasing. Of course, he was merely guarding his inheritance. He figured the only way to get it guaranteed was to marry her himself.

Maybe she should volunteer to marry the doctor. He didn't stir her senses the way Gabe did. He didn't tempt her to put her heart at risk. He didn't

make her want to seek out dark places so she could
have her way with him.

Nope, only Gabe did those things.

But Jeff seemed like a nice man.

"Katie," Gabe's insistent voice sounded in her
ear.

"Yes?"

"Where did you go? I spoke to you twice and
you didn't answer."

"I guess I was thinking. Why, what did you
want?"

"I was thinking it's time to go."

The sun had gone down and everyone was sitting
around chatting, playing with the babies. Katherine
had held Tuck and Alex's baby girl, delighting in
her sweetness. Mac and Samantha's oldest child,
Cassie, had toddled over to pat the baby's hand and
talk to Katherine.

They'd also eaten the desserts. Her cobbler had
been a big success. Jessica had even asked for a
meeting on Monday to discuss using it in the restaurant.

It had been a wonderful afternoon and evening.
Katherine didn't want it to end.

"Well, I certainly enjoyed myself. Thanks for
including me."

Gabe took her arm. "I'm riding with you."

She stared at him. "But you came with your father."

"He can follow me to your house."

"But Gabe, I'll be fine. There's no reason to—"

Gabe glared at Jeff, walking toward them, and muttered, "Oh, yes, there is."

When Jeff reached them, Gabe stuck out a hand. "Glad to visit with you, Jeff, but we've got to go."

"Yeah, me, too." His gaze traveled to the arm Gabe had around Katherine. "I didn't realize you two came together."

"We didn't. But we're going home together," Gabe returned in a firm voice. Clearly sending a male message.

"Gabe," Katherine protested. He'd sounded rude.

To her surprise, he bent his head and kissed her, there in the kitchen in front of everyone. "Katie," he said, mimicking her tone of voice.

Those around them laughed, and Katherine's cheeks flushed. What was wrong with the man? Was he setting the scene for their marriage so no one would suspect the truth? He was certainly doing a good job.

Once they'd said their goodbyes, he followed her out to the van she used for the bake shop.

"Now that you've made your point, you don't have to accompany me home," she said. It was important to keep a grasp on reality.

He opened the driver's door and escorted her into the van without saying a word. But before she could drive away, he'd circled the van and slid into the passenger side.

"Didn't you hear me?" she asked in frustration.

"Yeah, I did. But I'm going with you. We haven't had a chance to talk today."

"We talked all evening."

"Yeah, with Dr. Jeff hanging over your shoulder."

"He's a nice man."

"Keep away from him!"

"Gabe Dawson, you can't tell me what to do!"

He drew a deep breath, drumming his fingers on the dash. "Katie, look, we need to talk about our marriage."

His change of subject, when she'd just gotten up a good head of justified anger, took her breath away. She started the motor and began backing out of Tuck's driveway.

After she'd covered several miles without speaking, he tried again. "Katie, have you thought about it?"

"Yes." She couldn't say any more. She couldn't tell him she'd decided to give him what he wanted. At great risk to her happiness.

She thought about the babies she'd played with tonight. And about the babies she and Gabe could make if they were only a real couple. Her heart ached.

"Look, I don't know what to say to convince you, but I believe my grandmother wanted me to inherit. I don't know what bee got into her bonnet to make her pull such a trick."

"I do," Katherine whispered. Then she snapped her lips shut. How could she have been so careless? She wasn't prepared to tell Gabe that she'd confessed her love for him to his grandmother, after the failure of her own marriage.

"You do?"

"No! I mean, not really. I think she wanted you to settle in Cactus." That was certainly true enough.

"Well, I am. But I won't have anywhere to live if I don't inherit her house."

She glared at him. "Don't try that pity routine on me, Gabe Dawson! There are lots of places available. You could rent Jack's house. I think he's going to move in with Mom."

Gabe grinned. "Okay, so I was trying to play on your sympathy. But I love Gran's place."

"I know."

They were almost to her house. She needed to keep things calm just a couple of minutes longer. Then she could have more time to think about her decision. To be *sure* she could carry through with it. To prepare her resistance to the only man she'd ever loved.

"So, are you going to marry me?"

Of course, he wouldn't give her more time. Not a romantic proposal, either, but a good reminder that they weren't dealing in romance. Just practicalities.

"Yes," she said softly.

He didn't answer, and she wondered if he'd heard her. She looked at him and found him staring at her, as if in shock. "Have you changed your mind?"

"No! No, I haven't changed my mind, but I thought you were flirting with the doctor."

"I was not! I was being friendly."

"Yeah, right! If that was friendly—"

"Stop, Gabe Dawson. You've gotten what you wanted. But just because I'm marrying you for your inheritance, don't think you can tell me what to do!"

GABE'S HEART WAS THUMPING like a drum. He could scarcely think, much less carry on a conversation. "No, I wasn't trying to." Well, maybe he was.

But it didn't matter. She was going to marry him. "When?"

Her big blue gaze landed on him and then glanced away. "I don't know."

"I'd like it to be soon, to get everything settled." At least before two weeks was up and Jeff Hausen was back in town.

"I'm not sure."

"It will look better if we don't wait until the year is almost up. I don't want people to think—"

"I know. Alex explained."

He frowned. "Explained what?"

"That if we don't appear to be—that the charity Gran named might sue."

That hadn't occurred to him. But he didn't mind. He'd donate some money to the charity. It was only fair. Especially if that convinced Katie to marry him at once, to make their marriage appear normal.

As he intended it to be.

She pulled into her driveway, watching Will pull in behind them. After stopping the van, she said, "You'd better not keep your father waiting."

"Here's your hat, what's your hurry?" he said, glaring at her. "Are you trying to get rid of me?"

"No, but—"

Will appeared beside the passenger door. "Mind if I go say hello to Margaret?" he asked. "I haven't seen her in years."

"Of course not. Probably Jack Ledbetter is there, too, Will," Katie added. "I think that's his car. They're going to be married, soon."

"Really? But Jack is—I mean, I thought he was married?"

"He's a widower, Dad," Gabe told his father. "A couple of years now."

"Well, good for the two of them. I'll be out in a minute," he added over his shoulder as he strode to the house.

"When are they getting married?"

Katie seemed startled by his question. "They're going to have a small wedding next week."

He grinned as an idea hit him. "Great, come on." He opened the door and got out of the van.

"Gabe! Where are you—?"

He didn't answer her question, and he didn't stop. And he sure didn't consult her on his idea. He knew what her answer would be. He was planning on some help from the people inside.

He heard her get out of the van and grinned.

Reaching the back door before her, he knocked on it and then opened it.

"Margaret, may I come in?"

"Of course, Gabe, you know you're welcome,"

Margaret said, getting up to greet him. "Where's—?"

Katie appeared beside him. "What are you up to?"

"I'm visiting with your mom," he said calmly, ushering her in before him.

"Did you have fun this evening?" Margaret asked, a contented smile on her face.

"Yes, Mom, it was fun. You and Jack should have come."

"Maybe we will next time. We had a lot of plans to discuss before our marriage." Her cheeks bloomed with excitement, making her appear ten years younger.

Gabe watched as Katie smiled back. He hoped she kept smiling. "That's why we came in. We want to talk to you about your wedding."

"You do?" Margaret and Jack said in unison.

At the same time, Katie asked, "We do?" and frowned.

Gabe drew a deep breath. He was taking a little bit of a chance here, but he was in a hurry. "Yeah, we wondered if you'd mind a double wedding."

Margaret and Jack looked puzzled. His father's gaze flickered back and forth between him and Katie.

Katie glared at him.

"What do you mean?" Margaret asked.

"Katie and I are going to get married and we wanted—"

Margaret leaped to her feet and hurried over to hug her daughter, beaming at Gabe over her shoulder. "I'm so happy for you. Oh, yes, yes, a double wedding would be wonderful. Wouldn't it, Jack? You wouldn't mind, would you?"

She turned loose of Katherine and hurried back to the table to see if Jack agreed with her.

"Gabe Dawson, I'm going to kill you!" Katie muttered under her breath.

Jack, in the meantime, was answering Margaret's question. "Of course I don't mind, honey. It seems like a good idea."

Will, still watching Katherine and Gabe, said, "As long as Katie doesn't mind. Her wedding should be what she wants."

Gabe knew his father was hinting about his jumping the gun, but he'd known he was taking a risk. Hell, the worst risk was letting Katie fall in love with the damned doctor. He'd lost her ten years ago to duty. He wasn't going to lose her again.

Margaret looked at Will and then Katherine. "Dear, do you not want to have a double wedding? I thought—we can wait if you want to get married first."

"Hey!" Jack exclaimed. "But we planned—"

Margaret stared at him.

"Uh, well, whatever you want, Margaret," he finally said, his devotion to Margaret filling his gaze.

Jack's attitude, more than his father's words, affected Gabe. He grimaced and said, "I think I owe Katie an apology. I got carried away when she said she'd marry me. I didn't want to wait. But Dad's right, Katie. This is your decision.''

He was rewarded by Katie's glare disappearing. ''I hadn't thought about it, but you may be right, Gabe. It would certainly save a lot of work and expense.''

Will frowned. ''I'll take care of the expenses of the wedding, Katie. I don't want you to worry about that. After all, Gabe is my only son.'' He grinned. ''Oh, and by the way, welcome to the family.''

Gabe shot his father a grateful smile.

''Thank you, Will,'' Katie said, her voice sincere.

''Oh, this is so exciting,'' Margaret enthused. ''We've made a list of things to do. Why don't you look it over, Katie? We'll have to double the numbers, because you'll want to invite your friends, of course. I thought I'd ask Florence Greenfield to sing, and…''

Gabe put an arm around Katie. ''Maybe later, Margaret. I have a few things I need to discuss with Katie. Dad, can you give us a couple of minutes?''

He hoped his father understood his meaning. He couldn't afford to spend more than a couple of minutes with Katie at this point. Not with what he had in mind.

His father nodded.

Then Gabe pulled Katherine to the door.

Once it had closed behind them, she raised her chin. ''What do we need to discuss now? And isn't it a little late for discussion, since you've already made the decisions?''

"Sorry, Katie. I got carried away."

She glared at him but said nothing. Neither did he. He was afraid she'd hate his next idea even more.

"Well, what do we need to discuss?"

"Uh, I didn't exactly have discussion in mind. More like practice."

"Practice?"

"Yeah, for when the pastor says 'You may kiss the bride.'"

And he did.

Chapter Fourteen

Her world in a spin, Katherine wanted to hide away until the dust settled.

But she couldn't.

Monday, she met with Jessica.

"I think your new dessert is a perfect complement to the carrot cake. With a scoop of ice cream on it, it will be a huge success."

"Are you sure, Jessica? You're not offering to buy it because we're friends?" Katherine asked, less sure of herself as changes swirled around her.

Jessica stared at her. "Don't be silly, Katie! I don't make decisions about my business based on friendships. I tasted the cobbler Saturday, remember? It's going to be as big a success as the cake. Several ladies have asked for something lighter than the cake."

"Really? With the cobbler, you might offer two sizes of servings. A small dish might be very popular."

"Oh, good thinking. You're right. And it would be easier to vary the size with the cobbler." Jessica made some notes on the yellow pad in front of her. "Oh, your mom called and left a message for me. I haven't had time to call her back. Is there any problem about the reception Saturday?"

Katherine closed her eyes. She dreaded telling Jessica about the change of plans. She didn't want any searching questions about her emotional state. "Um, I think it's going to be larger than planned."

"But she reserved the entire room," Jessica pointed out, referring to the large room attached to the restaurant. On weekends, Jessica featured local bands there.

"I know. I think she just wanted to let you know."

"No problem. Did they decide to invite more people?"

Katherine chewed on her bottom lip. Finally she straightened her shoulders and lifted her chin. "Yes. You see, Gabe and I are joining them. I mean, we're doing a double wedding."

Jessica stared at her. Then she reached out and clasped Katherine's hand. "I'm so happy for you. I hope Cal and I are invited to the wedding?"

"Of course. Could you tell Melanie and Alex and Samantha? It's difficult to—to find time for everything."

"Of course, Katie. What else can I do to help?"

Katherine drew a deep breath. Friends were priceless, and Jessica was one of the best.

KATHERINE HAD PLANNED on baking her mother's wedding cake. Now it would also be her wedding cake. So she doubled the size and tried to find the time in her schedule to prepare it.

Ethel, her new employee, was doing an excellent job. She took a lot of work from Katie's shoulders. Since she and Jessica had come to an agreement about the cobbler, Katherine already had increased the workload.

Maybe she could clone Ethel.

"Katherine?" Ethel said hesitantly on Tuesday morning as they were preparing the carrot cakes.

"Yes?"

"I thought I should mention my sister, Alice. She said she'd like you to consider her when you want to hire more workers."

"Your sister? You have a sister who wants a job?" Katherine asked, her spirits rising. "Is she anything like you?"

"Yes. But everyone always considers her to be a better cook."

Since Ethel had turned out to be an excellent employee, Katherine felt sure her sister would do as well. "Tell her she's hired."

"Don't you want to interview her?" Ethel asked in surprise.

"Ethel, I don't have time to interview. Tell her to come in the morning. We'll have a trial run. If we're both satisfied, then we'll make it permanent. With the cobbler Jess wants, we'll have to have more help. Especially since she's calling the corporation in Dallas."

"You mean you may be making as many cobblers as you do cakes?'' Ethel asked in astonishment.

''No, at least not yet. We're only doing two cobblers a day for Jessica.'' Katherine sighed. Yes, her life was definitely spinning out of control.

The door to the serving area opened. ''Psst, Katherine!'' Mary whispered. ''He's here. Your fiancé.''

Word had certainly spread fast.

Katherine swallowed and drew a deep breath. ''I have to finish the cakes, Mary.''

''He said he just needed a minute.''

Katherine knew she wasn't going to convince anyone of her enthusiasm for the marriage if she hid in the kitchen. ''I'll be right back, Ethel.''

Her gaze found him at once, seated at a table for two, munching on a sausage roll. When he saw her, he stood and stepped forward to wrap his arms around her.

She stood stiffly in his embrace. ''Gabe! We're in public,'' she whispered.

A naughty grin on his face as soon as he'd brushed his lips across hers didn't denote any remorse. ''I know.''

''What did you want?'' She collapsed into the chair opposite the one he'd been using, afraid his touch was affecting her knees.

''A little more enthusiasm?'' he whispered, leaning toward her after sitting down.

She closed her eyes and prayed for strength and patience. ''Mornings are really busy around here.''

''Okay, okay. I wanted to meet you for lunch at The Last Roundup. Then I thought we'd go to Anderson's jewelry store. I understand he keeps a good stock since marrying is becoming so popular around here.''

Her mind wasn't functioning. Good stock? She knew Gabe didn't mean cattle, but then it hit her. "You mean buy a wedding ring?"

"No, an engagement ring." He grasped her left hand and played with her third finger. "We can pick out the wedding rings, too, but I want a ring on your finger now."

She blinked several times. Then she said, "That's not necessary. A plain gold band will be enough. Then, when it's over—"

"Hush!" Gabe ordered with a frown. "Never say that. Someone might overhear you. My fiancée will have an engagement ring."

"But the wedding is Saturday."

"Can you meet me for lunch?"

Apparently he'd decided not to discuss the ring issue anymore. "I won't be through here until about two. Why don't you go ahead with lunch, and I'll come to your office at two."

"I don't like you putting in so much time. You need to hire more help."

Katherine leaned back and stared at him. "I beg your pardon? I don't run my shop for entertainment, Gabriel Dawson. I have financial obligations."

"When we're married, I'll share those obligations."

Katherine thought she was going to lose her breakfast right there, which wouldn't do a lot for business. Clearly Gabe thought he'd offer her a financial reward for giving him his inheritance.

Springing to her feet, Katherine rushed for the door to the kitchen. She couldn't deal with this man or his plans right now.

He caught her at the door.

Pulling her against him, he lowered his mouth to hers and gave her another of those mind-blowing kisses. "I'll be back at two o'clock." Then he turned around and left the shop.

Katherine stood there staring after him until she realized everyone in the shop was staring in turn at her. Turning a bright red, she retreated to the kitchen.

GABE STRODE ACROSS the town square, his hands jammed in his pockets. He didn't want people to see his fists. He was so frustrated he wasn't sure he could manage.

She wouldn't even have lunch with him!

Well, damn it, after today, he'd have his ring on her finger. She'd belong to him. Sort of. And that was what frustrated him most of all.

Saturday they'd be married. But they wouldn't be married. At least not when the sun went down. How long would it take him to convince her their marriage had a chance? And what if he never convinced her?

Could he live with her, see her every day, pretend in public to be close to her, and not touch her when they went home? Every time he kissed her, he lost control.

Saturday night, on her back porch, he'd been ready to stretch out on the cement and make love to her. His father's voice had brought him out of his haze of sensuality.

He'd gotten the hell out of there before Katie could tell him to leave and never come back.

But who was going to stop him when they went home together?

"Morning, Gabe," Alex sang out as he entered the offices.

"What are you doing here this early?" Alex usually arrived around nine.

"I was up early throwing up and decided I might as well come in and get some work done. A nap sounds really good after lunch." She grinned at him and entered her office.

He followed her to the door. "Do you mind?"

"Mind what?"

"The pregnancy. I mean, you've got a successful career, and you already have one child. Did you want this baby?"

She raised one eyebrow and he started apologizing. "I shouldn't ask—"

"No, it's all right. The answer is yes, I want this baby. I'd like to have more, maybe two more. I love being a mother. And why not? I have it pretty easy. I get to work the hours I want. I have help at home. I have a loving husband and fantastic in-laws."

He shook his head and turned to go.

"Why did you ask?"

Gabe frowned, unsure what to say. But Alex had been honest with him. "I was thinking about Katie.

She's got a successful business, but it takes up a lot of her time. I wondered if she'd resent—I mean, should—'' He stopped, unable to voice his dreams.

"But I thought you two were, uh, meeting the terms of the will."

Gabe felt his cheeks heat up. "I'm hoping for more," he finally admitted.

"So she did agree to marry you? I heard a rumor."

"Surprise, surprise. Gossip in Cactus?" Gabe said, raising an eyebrow.

She ignored his sarcasm. "When?"

"Saturday."

"But that's when her mother and Jack Ledbetter—a double wedding?"

"Yeah."

"That's brilliant."

"Who's brilliant?" Mac asked from the hallway. Cal stood beside him.

"Gabe and Katie are having a double wedding with her mother on Saturday," Alex exclaimed.

"I know," Cal said casually.

Gabe and Alex stared at Cal, and Mac turned to look at his friend, too. Then Gabe asked, "How do you know? I hadn't told anyone yet."

"Katie told Jess yesterday because there'll be more guests at the reception, right? We're invited, right?"

"And she didn't call me?" Alex said, mock outrage in her voice.

"She was going to last night, but Ricky had a tummy ache. You know how she is. She held him all evening. Wouldn't even let me take over for a while." He grinned. "I don't know what we'll do when we have another one."

Alex's eyes widened even more. "You're expecting again, too?"

Both she and Mac congratulated Cal.

Gabe felt envy. He wanted a family, too. But he didn't hesitate to congratulate his friends.

"It's too early to be sure, but you know Jess. She's absolutely sure."

Alex clasped her hands together. "Oh, it's wonderful. Now our baby will have someone to play with." Then her eyes widened even more. "I've got to call Melanie. I bet she and Spence are thinking the same thing. Sam and Mac won't be the only ones with two children." She sent her partner a triumphant smile.

"Hey, don't say anything yet," Cal warned, an anxious look on his face. "She'll kill me. You have to promise to act surprised when she tells you."

"Cal Baxter, you weren't supposed to tell?" Alex asked, outrage in her voice. "I don't know what kind of sheriff you are when you can't even keep your new baby a secret!"

"Hey, I'm a good sheriff!"

Gabe decided he'd better intervene. "You're the best, Cal. I understand how it could slip out. Because you're so happy about the new baby, right?"

"Yeah, that's it. And you'll all pretend not to know?" he asked anxiously.

"Sure," Gabe said, and then looked at the other two.

"Sure," Mac agreed.

"Well...I suppose," Alex added.

Gabe hurriedly said, "And you're all invited to the wedding on Saturday. Will you be there?" That should change the subject.

They all agreed.

"I'm going to have my dad as my best man. Oh, and he's renting Jack Ledbetter's place."

The men all commented about that piece of information, but Alex had girl things on her mind. "I have to talk to Katie and see if she needs to take a shopping trip into Lubbock. We could go this afternoon."

"What about your nap?" Gabe asked.

"It can wait."

"Well, actually, I'm meeting her at two to buy her engagement ring. I don't think she'll have time today." And he wasn't going to put off getting the ring.

"Good idea," Cal said. "I didn't like the way that doctor was following her around."

"He's a nice man," Mac said. "Sam is impressed with his credentials."

Gabe frowned at his friend as if he'd betrayed him. "Katie's mine!"

Mac raised both hands. "Hey, I'm not arguing that. But Sam said—"

"I don't care if he's the best doctor in the world. I don't want him hanging around Katie." He glowered at all of them.

"Calm down, son," Cal said, clapping him on

the shoulder. "The lady's agreed, so you're home free."

Gabe knew differently. But one day. He wasn't going to give up. And the first step was putting a ring on her finger.

"DID YOU EAT LUNCH?"

Katherine turned startled eyes on Gabe as he asked his question, leaning against the doorjamb, his arms crossed over his chest.

She'd planned to meet him at his office. What was he doing here? "I was going to come to your office."

"You haven't answered my question."

She rolled her eyes. What was wrong with the man? "I eat all day long. I work in a kitchen. Are you afraid I'll dry up and blow away?"

His gaze roamed her figure and Katherine felt her body heat up. Damn, Gabe Dawson could still turn her inside out with a look. He always had had that talent.

"Come on. Let's go," he finally said, abandoning his questioning.

"Let me wash up." She hadn't worn her uniform today because she hadn't been waiting on customers. With Ethel's sister Alice starting tomorrow, if things worked out, she might be able to remain in the kitchen all the time.

When she came to Gabe's side, he took her hand and headed outside, waving goodbye to Evelyn and Mary.

"Are we in a hurry?" she asked as he pulled her along.

"Sorry. I didn't mean to rush you, but I'm looking forward to putting a ring on your finger."

She blinked several times, thinking about his words. Why? While the marriage would bring him his inheritance, an engagement would do nothing for him. "But it's the marriage that counts."

"Uh, yeah."

They'd crossed the square and reached Anderson's jewelry store, so Katherine didn't pursue the mystery of why the ring was so important to Gabe. The shop was empty when they entered, but the bell on the door alerted Mr. Anderson, and he came from his office.

"Good afternoon. I was wondering if I'd be seeing the two of you," he said with a big smile.

"Cactus gossip at work, I suppose," Gabe returned. "Since you know why we're here, what have you got to show us?"

"I have a wide array of choices. I need to know what you have in mind. A ring set? A gold band? Two matching rings?"

Katherine opened her mouth to suggest a solitary gold band. Before she could get the words out, Gabe took charge.

"I want a nice diamond engagement ring, with a matching wedding ring and a gold band for me."

Mr. Anderson stared at Gabe, as if asking a silent question. Whatever he saw in Gabe's expression must have been an answer he liked. "I see. Well, now, I have a special group of rings in my office. I'll be right back.''

Katherine tugged on Gabe's hand, still holding hers. ''Gabe,'' she whispered, ''there's no need to spend a lot of money. A plain band will mean just as much as something expensive. You'll still get your inheritance.''

''I don't want people to think I'm not proud of my wife,'' he assured her, staring into her eyes.

''But—''

''Here we go. These are the finest rings I carry. Let's see if any of them fit your needs,'' Mr. Anderson said, setting a black velvet tray on the glass counter.

Katherine drew in her breath at the beauty of the jewelry. Normally she didn't wear rings, because she'd only have to remove them when she worked. But she admitted to herself that she loved wearing them.

Gabe surveyed the selection and chose a diamond solitaire with a particularly brilliant shine. He took Katherine's hand and slid the ring onto her third finger. It was a perfect fit.

''What do you think?'' he asked softly.

''It's beautiful, but I think it's too big.''

''Three carats,'' Mr. Anderson said promptly. ''And of a particularly fine quality. In fact, Gabe, you've got quite an eye. That's the finest diamond I have, though not quite the largest.''

''It fits you,'' Gabe pointed out.

''We can size any of the rings,'' Mr. Anderson inserted. ''Some people don't like the traditional rings, so I have some colored stones mixed in.'' He pointed out a sapphire surrounded by diamonds.

Gabe smiled but said, ''We're traditional people, Mr. Anderson. I'll buy my wife other rings if she wants them, but for our wedding rings, we want traditional.''

''Well, you've made an excellent choice.''

''And the wedding band that goes with it?''

Gabe took the band the man handed him and showed it to Katherine, but he didn't put it on her finger.

''Shouldn't I try it on?''

''It's the same size as the engagement ring. It'll fit.''

''Are you going to wear a ring?'' she asked softly. They hadn't really discussed that point.

''Oh, yeah,'' Gabe said, grinning at her.

She was becoming more and more confused. Why was he so enthusiastic about appearing to be married? Was it all part of the window dressing Alex had thought was necessary? If so, he was doing a great job.

He tried on several wedding bands until he found one they both liked. When Katherine tried to pay for his ring, he insisted they all be charged to his account.

Katherine stood her ground. ''No. *I* want to pay for your wedding band.''

''That *is* the traditional way,'' Mr. Anderson said helpfully.

A smile slowly spread across Gabe's face. ''Then

that's the way we'll handle it, because this marriage is going to be traditional all the way through.''

It occurred to Katherine that she had a lot of questions to ask Gabe Dawson, like what did he mean by that statement?

Chapter Fifteen

Gabe didn't want to answer questions.

Katherine was frantically busy the rest of the week, but she could have made time to have a long talk with her fiancé. If he'd shown any inclination to talk.

But, if anything, he avoided her.

Which didn't bode well for their "traditional" marriage.

She made a shopping trip into Lubbock with Alex and Melanie. Jessica planned to go, but she had to go to Dallas for a last-minute meeting with the TGM Corporation with whom she consulted on a regular basis.

Katherine found a beautiful wedding gown that fit her perfectly with the exception of the hem. The shop promised to have the hem shortened by Friday. She added a fingertip veil and satin shoes, determined to look the traditional bride.

"How are you going to wear your hair?" Melanie asked. "Will you wear it down? It's so beautiful."

"Do you think it will look right, hanging down my back?" Katherine asked. "Maybe I should get it cut?"

Both Melanie and Alex shook their heads.

"I think Gabe would kill us if we let that happen," Alex assured her.

Katherine stared at Alex, a question in her eyes. It wasn't the first comment Alex had made that implied Gabe had more than a monetary interest in his bride. He couldn't possibly have convinced Alex that their marriage was anything other than what it was. She knew the truth.

"Who's going to give you away?" Melanie asked, distracting Katherine.

"Joe's giving Mom away and Paul is going to give me away. That sounds so old-fashioned, doesn't it? Giving me away."

"It sounds traditional," Alex said.

"You sound like Gabe," Katherine protested. Any reminder of her groom made her nervous. As the wedding drew closer, she fought the dream that her marriage was real. It would be too easy to believe…until their divorce. Then she'd be heartbroken.

"Are Diane, Raine and Susan going to be bridesmaids?"

"Yes, so we have to find them dresses, too. I have their sizes," Katherine added.

The bridal shop consultant showed them what they had available in those sizes. Katherine was immediately drawn to a royal-blue satin dress that would complement all three of her sisters. "Do you like this one?"

"It's gorgeous," Melanie assured her, and Alex nodded in agreement.

"If they carried pink rosebud bouquets, it would be perfect," Alex added. "Very traditional."

Katherine had trouble swallowing. That word kept coming up.

"Okay, we'll take them," she told the saleslady.

"Do you want to pick them up on Friday, or take them with you?"

"We'll take them with us. If they have to be altered, we'll get someone locally to do the work."

When they got back to Cactus, Katherine went home, anxious to show the bridesmaid gowns to Susan. Raine and Diane wouldn't be home until Friday night.

She found a message from Jessica waiting for her, but there was also one from the corporation that ran the restaurants in Amarillo.

For once, she was distracted from thoughts of her upcoming wedding. She called Jessica first. "Jess? It's Katherine. You called?"

"Yes. The meeting went very well today. I don't know if they'll call today—"

"They've left word. But I thought I'd call you first to see what was going on. Are the cakes not doing well?"

Jessica laughed. "You worrywart. The cakes are outperforming their expectations. They want them in all their restaurants."

"But that would be impossible!" Katherine

cried. She was pleased they were working out, but she couldn't possibly make enough cakes to supply the eighteen or twenty restaurants, or get them delivered to insure freshness.

"I know. I told them. That's when they decided to buy your recipe from you."

Katherine gasped. "Buy my recipe? But—"

"I know. But they'll pay you handsomely. And I told them about the cobbler. They'll probably be out to taste it soon. They were intrigued by the sound of it."

"Jessica, thank you so much. You've been such a good friend. If they pay me a lump sum for the recipe, I can make sure Paul and Susan get their schooling. Oh, this is wonderful!"

"I'm glad. Of course, you wouldn't have to worry about that anyway since you're marrying Gabe. After all, he's got lots of money, and I know he'd help you."

Katherine wasn't going to allow Gabe to assume her family responsibilities as payment. She didn't want to be paid. "It's important that *I* take care of my family."

"Call the office and see what they offer," Jessica said, not responding to her statement. "And let me know what you decide. And Katie, you don't have to decide today. Tell them you'll have to discuss it with your lawyer."

Katherine did as Jessica suggested. She was glad, because the initial numbers tossed out were so big she couldn't think.

After talking to Jessica, she called Alex at home

and made an appointment the next morning to discuss the contract and the payment.

She was still talking to Alex when her mother called her from the kitchen. "That's Mom calling. I'll see you in the morning," she told Alex, hung up the phone and flew to the kitchen to tell her mother the good news.

Only to find Gabe waiting for her.

"The shopping trip was that good?" he asked as he took in her beaming face.

"Oh! Oh, yes, it was fine."

Gabe narrowed his gaze. "It wasn't the shopping trip that put that smile on your face, was it?"

Katherine let her gaze flicker between Margaret and Gabe. "No, actually. I had some good news."

"What is it, dear?" Margaret asked, her expression eager.

"Mom, the corporation wants to buy my carrot cake recipe." She named the figure initially offered and Margaret almost passed out.

"For a recipe? Oh, my. Oh, my."

"Sit down, Margaret," Gabe insisted, leading her mother to a chair.

"It means I can provide college for Paul and Susan without any problem," Katherine added. "And I can—"

"You don't have to worry about them," Gabe said, interrupting her. "I'm setting up college funds for them."

"No! They're my family, my responsibility," she said, her voice tightening.

"But after Saturday, they'll be my family, too."

She couldn't argue that, not in front of her mother. She didn't want her mother to know that their marriage would end a year after Mrs. Dawson's death. That's when the terms of the will would be fulfilled.

Margaret laughed with joy. "Maybe one of you should set up scholarship funds for your own children, and the other for Paul and Susan. Then everyone will be taken care of."

Katie turned a bright pink. Even the thought of children, with Gabe as their father, brought heartache because it could never be.

However, it provided a way out.

"Good idea, Gabe," Katherine said staunchly, daring him to disagree, "you provide for our children and I'll provide for my sister and brother."

The look in his eyes gave her pause. What was he thinking?

"Okay, sweetheart," he said, his voice warm. "And how many children should I prepare for? Two? Six? A dozen?"

Margaret laughed. "After you have a couple, you can make that decision. It's amazing how time-consuming children can be."

"Mom's right. It's a little early to decide how many, since we're not even married." Katherine turned her back on Gabe, unwilling to discuss babies with him anymore. "What can I do to help with dinner, Mom?"

It was Gabe who answered. "I thought I'd take you out for dinner this evening. All the gang are meeting at The Last Roundup tonight."

"Who do you mean?"

"Cal, Spence, Tuck, Mac, and Rick Astin and his wife. Maybe a couple of more. Cal called and asked us to join them."

She should have known. Gabe had worked at not being alone with her this week. He wouldn't have asked her to dinner if the invitation hadn't come from someone else. And there was no possibility of discussing their "marriage" in all that company.

"That sounds like fun. Shall I meet you at the restaurant? What time?"

"I'll swing by and pick you up. We're meeting at seven," Gabe said. "That gives you plenty of time to get ready."

"You needn't make it sound like I'll need all that time!" Katherine snapped, irritation suddenly rising in her.

Margaret stared at her daughter. "Katie! What's wrong with you? Gabe didn't—"

"It's okay, Margaret," Gabe said, patting her on the arm. "I think it's pre-wedding nerves. Aren't you a little jittery this week, too?"

That dazed look of joyous wonder came over Margaret's face. Katherine had gotten used to the look whenever her mother thought about Jack Ledbetter. "Oh, no. I can't wait."

Gabe stared at her mother, then turned to look at Katherine. For a second, Katherine thought she read envy in his gaze. But he looked away, and she couldn't be sure. Besides, he didn't want her love and devotion. He only wanted his inheritance.

She lifted her chin and nodded in his direction.

"Sorry I snapped at you. I'll be ready a little before seven."

He accepted her dismissal without comment and turned to go.

"Um, I'll be back in a minute," Margaret suddenly said and scurried from the kitchen.

Katherine was embarrassed by her mother's obvious attempt to leave them alone for a private goodbye. She could have told her it wasn't necessary.

"Is something wrong with your mother?" Gabe asked, a puzzled look on his handsome face.

"No. Have you invited your mother to the wedding?"

Gabe grinned. "Yeah. She was outraged and refused to come."

"I'm sorry."

"I'm not. I've finally realized how much she has interfered in my life. And how miserable she's made my dad. It doesn't concern me if she chooses not to participate in any part of my life."

"But she is your mother."

"Yeah, but Gran was more a mother to me than Mom. And Gran will be at our wedding, in spirit, with a big smile on her face. That will be enough for me."

Tears filled Katherine's eyes at the memory of Gran and how much she'd meant to her.

"Hey, don't cry," Gabe said, moving closer, reaching out as if he meant to touch her. Then he snatched his hand back to his side. "Uh, Gran really liked you."

She almost told him then why Gran had written those conditions into her will. She felt so guilty about them. But she kept silent. After all, she was doing what she could to make things right. "I loved her," she said simply.

"Yeah," Gabe responded quietly. Then he cleared his throat. "I'd better go." He backed his way to the door, his gaze fixed on her, as if waiting for something.

Katherine watched him, fighting the desire for a goodbye like he'd given her Saturday night. A kiss that had taken her back ten years, when life had been so much simpler, and so much sweeter.

He reached for the door just as Susan opened it. "Oh, sorry, Gabe, I didn't mean to bump into you," her sister said with a grin. "I didn't expect to see you here now. Oh, Katie, you're home early. I guess that explains him," she said, nodding her head in Gabe's direction.

Susan, with the assurance that her home life would be secure, had become happier in the past few days. Besides, she was excited to have Gabe as part of the family.

Gabe excused himself to Susan and bolted from the house, as if he were being chased by demons.

"Did I interrupt a fight?" Susan asked, alarm in her voice.

"No, and I bought the bridesmaid dresses today. Come see if you approve." Katherine knew that topic would distract her sister from impossible questions.

GABE, DRESSED IN pressed jeans, a white shirt and a tweed sports coat, said good-night to his father as he left the house. "I'm not sure when I'll be home, Dad."

Will grinned. "I don't think I've waited up for you since you turned eighteen, son."

Gabe grinned. "Yeah, but you haven't experienced Cinnamon when it's bedtime. She won't stay by herself."

"No problem. She's a sweet pup."

"I'm glad you think so, because you'll have to keep an eye on her while we're on our honeymoon." His mind on the honeymoon, he almost left without another word. Then he thought to ask, "What are your plans for the night?"

"They're having a forty-two tournament at the Baptist church. I'm going to go play a few hands."

"Good for you. I didn't realize you liked dominoes that much," Gabe said, looking curiously at his father.

"Your mother didn't think it was fashionable. I spent a lot of boring evenings at the opera."

With a grin, he wished his father an enjoyable evening and escaped to his car. At least his change of life hadn't worsened his father's. Will seemed relieved that he no longer lived with his wife.

Gabe had offered his mother the chance to reunite with her family, at least temporarily, when he called and invited her to the wedding. Her reaction had been totally self-centered and rude.

Gabe's jaw squared. He would never intentionally harm his mother, but he also would never allow her to harm Katie. And her attitude toward the woman he loved would be painful.

His heartbeat sped up at the thought of Katie. The love he'd once felt for her had never been forgotten. Having gone underground in his heart, it appeared to have grown stronger through the years. Now that he'd finally acknowledged that love, it had spread all through him, making it almost impossible to be in her company without touching her.

Which was why he'd been avoiding her this week.

He could only put up so much resistance.

What would he do after they were married?

Work long hours. Read a lot of books. Maybe ride that new gelding he'd bought. An immediate picture of him and Katie sharing a moonlight ride had him reminding himself that he needed to find activities for one, not two.

By the time he reached Katie's house, he was feeling strong, determined, sure he could manage his libido.

Until she walked out of the house.

Damn, he wanted her.

Not just her body. He wanted to know her thoughts, her concerns, to share her joys. He wanted to feel her beside him, to share her life in every way.

He slid from behind the wheel and met her as she walked to his car. With his resistance all gone, he wrapped his arms around her and kissed her, their mouths melding into a rush of emotions that carried them high above their difficulties.

When she finally pulled back, her heavy breathing matching his own, she whispered, "You shouldn't—"

"I thought someone might be watching," he hurriedly said. "We want everyone to think it's for real. In case the charity sues," he added for good measure. He was thankful for Alex's warning to Katie.

Katie licked her lips as she pushed away from him and Gabe almost groaned.

"We'd better go. We don't want to be late."

Hell, no, he was dying to spend the evening with old friends, unable to even talk to Katie, much less touch her. It would be a rare evening of torture. He couldn't wait.

Their dinner party turned out to be an impromptu shower for the new couple. Only instead of serious presents, his and Katie's friends brought them impractical, suggestive items. Like a baby-name book, for planning ahead. A sheer nightgown that would tempt a saint, especially when Gabe imagined Katie inside it.

They even provided some silk briefs for him.

Katherine's cheeks turned a bright pink, which lit Gabe up even more. Was she doing some imagining on her own? He hoped so. He shouldn't be the only one to suffer.

There were questions about the honeymoon, which brought Katie's gaze to him. He read her questions in her eyes, but he refused to satisfy anyone's curiosity about what they were doing after the wedding. He and Jack Ledbetter had talked and worked out a plan.

Their evening ended surprisingly early. By ten o'clock, he had Katie back at her house. But not safely inside it.

"I need to go in," she said, holding the door handle as soon as he shut off the engine.

"Not yet," he said, reaching for her arm to insure she cooperated.

"Did you want to say something?"

"No! No, but your family is going to expect us to take a little time for ourselves. Otherwise, they'll think we've argued." That excuse seemed as logical as anything he could come up with.

"I'll tell them I need to get my sleep. I have to be at work at six, you know." She actually scooted closer to the door, on the outer edge of the leather seat.

"Relax, Katie, I'm not going to attack you," he growled.

"Of course not." Then she sat up a little straighter. "What did you mean when you mentioned a honeymoon?"

Damn! He hadn't wanted to discuss his plans. "It's a secret."

"So you said, but don't you think *I* should know what you've planned? I certainly can't leave on a moment's notice, and anyway, it would be pointless."

Gabe didn't appreciate that term being applied to his honeymoon. Okay, so she had a point. A honeymoon was for two people to be alone, to—well, to be alone. And he couldn't risk that.

"It would look strange to have no honeymoon. After all, I'm not short of money."

"We can use my business as an excuse. I can't be away. I have contracts to honor. And I'm going to be negotiating my contract about the recipe. And they want to taste my new cobbler, the one Jessica—"

"It's a wonder you can even spare the time to walk down the aisle," he snapped.

She glared at him. "I have to secure my family's future. They won't disappear just because I'll be married for a few months."

"Damn it, Katie! I won't leave you destitute!" He had no intention of leaving her at all, but he couldn't tell her that.

"I will not take money from you for doing what I think is right! I'm marrying you for Gran's sake. It would be wrong for you to pay me."

Just what a guy liked to hear. The woman he desperately loved was marrying him because she loved his *grandmother*. Not good for the ego.

"We'll work things out. But I'm planning on a short trip, for appearance's sake. We'll leave Saturday afternoon and return on Wednesday evening. Your mom and Jack are going to leave Thursday morning."

"What? They're going to wait until Thursday for their honeymoon? But that's wrong. At least they'll enjoy theirs!" Then Katie looked away, her cheeks flaming.

Gabe drew in a deep breath, forcing away thoughts of what it would take for him to enjoy a honeymoon with Katie. "Your mom was worried about leaving Susan and Paul home alone. They're good kids, but even good kids can get in trouble without any supervision. When we get back, she and Jack are going to Hawaii for two weeks."

"Two weeks? That will be expensive," Katie said, frowning, nibbling on her bottom lip.

Gabe swallowed as he fought the urge to help her nibble. "Uh, it's my wedding present to them for letting us horn in on their wedding."

"And Jack accepted? That's ridiculous. I'll talk to him and—"

"Don't you dare mess up my arrangements!" Gabe shouted. Drawing a deep breath, hoping to regain his calm, he said, "I worked long and hard to convince him. If you want to contribute, buy your mother a trousseau. And I'm only paying for the airfare and hotel. Jack will be spending a lot of money on other things."

To his surprise, Katie leaned toward him, her blue eyes filled with tears. "You're right, Gabe. That's very generous of you. Mom always wanted to go to Hawaii. I'm sorry I was so rude." Then she kissed him on the cheek.

Like a strong dam weakened by a little crack, Gabe's resistance crumbled at that small touch. His arms shot out and pulled her body to him, his lips finding hers.

Chapter Sixteen

Gabe's father stood just behind him, as one of Jack's friends held the same position behind Jack. They all watched as the three younger Peters girls glided down the aisle in their royal blue gowns, each carrying a bouquet of pink rosebuds.

To Gabe's surprise, the church was filled with townspeople. Many of his father's old friends, as well as Margaret and Jack's, were there. Then the younger contingent represented his and Katie's friends.

As Diane, the oldest of Katie's sisters, reached the candlelit altar, the organ music changed. Gabe drew a deep breath as Katie appeared at the back of the church, on Paul's arm. Her golden hair, usually braided, was loose, flowing down her back, topped by a fingertip veil that gave her a misty, romantic look. Her gown, in white satin, made her look like a fairy princess.

More beautiful than ever.

Despair filled Gabe. How would he ever control himself? And if he didn't, would he lose her forever? Wednesday night, he'd had her half-undressed, seeking the exquisite pleasure he'd once found with her, when she'd called a halt, escaping from his touch.

They'd scarcely talked since.

He'd hidden for several days, afraid if she saw him she'd cancel the wedding.

But here she was, looking like the culmination of all his dreams…and his nightmares. Ecstasy…just out of reach.

His father's hand fell on his shoulder, as if he'd felt his son's dilemma. Gabe hoped not. He'd tried to act the role of an eager bridegroom. Not hard to do as long as he pretended tonight would allow him to hold Katie close, to show her his love, to begin a life together that would last forever.

She and Paul reached the altar. She stared at the minister, refusing to meet Gabe's gaze. Paul gave him a nervous grin, but Gabe didn't find that sign of friendship nearly as essential as Katie's acknowledgment of his presence.

Maybe she'd refuse to take her vows. Maybe she'd be a runaway bride, unable to fulfill her promise at the last minute. Maybe she'd denounce him in front of God and everyone.

Margaret next appeared, in a silk suit, looking sophisticated and charming, younger than she had a right to. Gabe figured Katie would look much the same when she turned fifty, too. Still turning him on.

He couldn't imagine a time when he wouldn't want to hold her.

When the minister began their vows, Gabe accepted that Katie was going to go through with the wedding. He held her cold hand in his and solemnly repeated the words linking them together before man and God.

Then the minister got to the best part. "You may kiss your brides."

Gabe figured he'd better enjoy himself. It might be the last opportunity he'd have for a long time.

KATHERINE LEANED against Gabe's strong body, letting him guide their steps as they took the traditional dance, along with Margaret and Jack, at the reception.

She could indulge her fantasy of a real marriage as long as she was surrounded by friends and family.

As if he read her thoughts, Gabe's arms tightened, pulling her even closer. He whispered, "We dance like we've done this forever. We fit together perfectly."

She remembered thinking those same thoughts when he'd escorted her to a spring dance, ten years ago. She'd been so proud of her escort, a college senior. Incredibly handsome.

Instead of answering, she buried her face in his neck.

"Katie? Are you okay?"

"Fine," she muttered, but she didn't raise her head.

He turned loose her hand and wrapped his other

arm around her also, barely moving on the dance floor. She was completely in his embrace.

Like Wednesday night when he'd kissed her in his car. She'd barely escaped with her secret intact. She loved him. But she couldn't tell him without total embarrassment. Certainly not then, before the wedding. He might even have sacrificed his inheritance to avoid being saddled with a wife who didn't want a divorce.

No bachelor wanted someone hanging on him, asking for more than he wanted to give.

Oh, Gabe wanted sex. Alex was right about that. A man didn't turn down free sex. But it wouldn't be free if it carried the price of forever.

Since Wednesday Katherine had done a lot of thinking. Their marriage wouldn't work as long as this strong attraction had to be fought. They'd drive each other crazy and wear themselves out fighting the temptation.

So, either they lived in separate towns, maybe separate states, which wasn't a possibility, or they gave in to the temptation.

And broke her heart.

She'd realized, however, that her heart was going to be broken anyway. So she'd made a decision.

Tonight she would seduce her husband.

For the year she'd been granted, she would make love to Gabe whenever possible. And when it ended, she'd have memories to last a lifetime, to ease her despair.

Because she knew, from the past, that she'd

never find another man to replace him in her heart or her bed.

The only thing she had resolved to deny herself was a baby. She wanted Gabe's child more than anything. But she didn't want to deny that child his father. She didn't want to force Gabe to choose between his freedom and his baby. She didn't want him to think she was trying to trap him.

Like his mother had his father.

She wouldn't do that to him.

So she'd gone to Brockmeier's drugstore and purchased a supply of condoms. And she'd gone to Samantha for a prescription for birth control pills. Sam had warned her that they wouldn't be effective for a month.

"Sweetheart," Gabe whispered in her ear. "The music has stopped."

She lifted her head and drew his down to her so she could kiss him. He had no problem with her behavior since he immediately took control. Until she feared he'd forget where they were.

"Hey, pal, no consummation on the dance floor," Cal warned, slapping Gabe on the back. "It's against the law. You'd end up spending your first night of wedded bliss in the slammer. Alone."

While Jessica chastised Cal for his words, Katherine gathered her emotions, promising herself that later tonight she wouldn't have to do so. At least she would have his physical love.

GABE WAS GRATEFUL to Cal for his intervention. He needed distance from Katie, not more closeness.

He'd made reservations for them at the Broadmoor, a famous hotel in Colorado Springs. They'd spend a couple of hours of their first night on an airplane.

They were staying in the bridal suite. He figured that meant he'd be occupying the couch. He hoped it was a long one. Not that he'd be spending much time on it. He knew he'd be pacing the living room, trying to think of anything but the woman in the next room.

And not succeeding.

Cal swept Katie across the floor in a lively polka. Gabe realized Jessica was waiting for him to follow with her. "Sorry, Jess, I got lost for a minute. Dance?"

"I'd love to, but not as energetically as Cal is. I don't know if he's told you, but I'm expecting again."

Gabe schooled his features to show surprise. "Really? Well, congratulations. That's terrific."

"We'll see if you think the same thing when your wife throws up every morning," Jessica said, but her grin told him she thought the baby was worth the discomfort.

"I can't wait," he murmured, picturing Katie with her stomach swollen with his child.

Jessica sighed. "I know. When Mabel and the other matchmakers were so focused on getting grandchildren, I thought they were a little over the top. But once I held our son in my arms, I understood completely."

"Yeah," Gabe agreed, his voice husky. How long would it take to convince Katie their marriage was real? How long before he could hope for a child, a joint pledge of their love. He wouldn't consider a baby before he'd convinced her of his love, of the permanence of their marriage.

He wouldn't do to her what his mother had done.

Use a child as a bargaining chip.

But he longed to hold his child, and his wife, in his arms. He cleared his throat again. "How many children do you and Cal want?"

Jessica gave him a dreamy smile. "I don't know. We're taking it one baby at a time. I hope we have a girl this time."

His smile matched Jessica's as he pictured a little girl like Katie, long blond curls, that sweet smile on her face. That naughty twinkle in her eye.

The music ended and Gabe looked for Katie. He needed to hold her.

But the only time he got close to her for the next hour was when they cut the incredibly beautiful cake she'd made for her own wedding.

Then it was time to leave. They had an hour's drive into the Lubbock airport and a two-hour flight to Colorado Springs. Katie's bag had been put in the trunk of his car by Paul earlier, so they were ready to go.

He was more than ready.

"WE'RE GOING TO Colorado Springs?" Katie asked when they reached the gate at the airport.

"Yeah, to the Broadmoor. It's a beautiful place. Lots of things to do there."

She only had one activity in mind, and that thought had her blushing a bright red.

"You don't like our destination?" he asked, an anxious look on his face that pleased her.

"I think it will be wonderful," she assured him. But she wished they were going somewhere closer. With a bed. She was amazed at her thoughts. She'd only enjoyed sex once. With Gabe. The only other man she'd had sex with, Darrell, had seemed clumsy and inconsiderate. She'd hated his touching her.

Now she could scarcely control her desire, eager to once again find happiness in Gabe's arms. Temporary happiness. That thought dimmed her anticipation, but she shoved it away.

If God only gave her a year in Gabe's life, she was going to make the most of it. She was going to smile and let him go when the time came. She pressed her lips together and nodded, determination filling her.

"Katie? They're boarding. Are you okay?"

She tested out her smile. "I'm fine. How about you?"

He didn't look quite as happy as her, but he nodded. "I'm fine, too."

THE CAB RIDE TO THE HOTEL wasn't that long. Gabe wished he was more tired than he was. It would make it easier to fall asleep on that blasted couch. The one he had yet to see but already hated.

The staff at the Broadmoor, when they arrived, were efficient and discreet, not embarrassing the newlyweds but still eager to make their visit a happy one.

Gabe figured he shouldn't tell them their efforts would be wasted.

When they reached the bridal suite, the bellhop looked at him expectantly as he swung open the door. Gabe, who'd tried to avoid touching Katie since they'd left Texas, to build up his resistance again, had no choice but to swing her into his arms.

Her hands went behind his neck and she smiled up at him like the blushing bride she was supposed to be. He swallowed the lump in his throat. He wanted to observe all the rituals, because he didn't intend to allow her another marriage. But it was damn hard since he knew those rituals would stop at the bedroom door.

No traditional wedding night for him.

Even as they entered, a second bellhop arrived with a bottle of champagne in a silver ice bucket and a tray of chocolate-dipped strawberries and cheese and crackers.

"Compliments of the hotel, sir," the bellboy announced, a wide smile on his face. "In case you work up an appetite."

Gabe saw Katie's face turn bright red. He hurriedly gave both men a tip and escorted them to the door.

When he turned around, Katie was coming out of the bedroom. "It's a beautiful suite, Gabe," she told him.

He was a little surprised. He had figured Katie

would be running away from him, not coming toward him.

"Uh, yeah. Do you want some of this food? The meal on the airplane wasn't too tasty."

She moved to the tray and Gabe realized his mistake. He was standing beside it, which made Katie much too close to him. He crossed to the window. "You can see the Rockies from here," he assured her. Not too bright since the city was located right at the base of the mountains.

Katie chuckled. He whirled around because the laughter had sounded right behind him. He hadn't expected to find her beside him again.

She held up a half-eaten strawberry. "I had a bite. Now it's your turn."

The thought of putting his mouth where hers had been, of tasting the same fruit, was more erotic than he'd expected. He shoved away from her, striding across to their bags. "Uh, no, I don't care for strawberries."

This time she didn't follow him.

He turned back to see a look of sadness on her face that almost brought him to his knees. Scrambling for something to distract her, he said, "You want a turn in the bathroom first?"

It worked. She drew a deep breath and the sad look disappeared, replaced by such determination that he was puzzled. "Yes, thank you."

"I'll carry your bag into the—in here." Man, he had it bad when he couldn't even say the word *bedroom*. He set her bag down and hurried into the living room before she could even enter. He didn't want to be in the same room with her and a bed.

He just didn't trust himself.

Turning on the television to drown out any sounds, like water splashing on her body as she stripped and took a shower, he tried to concentrate on something other than Katie.

And, of course, failed miserably.

When the bedroom door opened and she asked if he wanted the bathroom now, his sprawled body jerked into rigidity. "Uh, thanks, but I've gotten involved in this movie. You go on to bed. I'll, uh, watch it."

Silence met his words, and he was forced to look over his shoulder. Katie stood in the doorway wearing a sheer blue nightgown that enhanced her eyes and revealed her body more than he could have imagined.

"Katie!" he exclaimed, his voice strangulated. Dear Lord, how was he supposed to resist that vision?

"Yes, Gabe? You're more interested in a movie than you are me?"

He forced his gaze away and grabbed a pillow from the sofa to hold in his lap. "You don't want me more interested in you, Katie. You're being a tease and I don't appreciate it."

More silence.

Then he heard a weary sigh. "No, Gabe, I'm not being a tease. I'm just going about this the wrong way."

"This?" He kept his gaze averted, hoping he could convince his body to forget what he'd seen.

"This…seduction. I should have explained."

Seduction. *Seduction?* He shot up from the couch. "What are you talking about?"

"I made a decision. But I forgot to include you in the discussion."

"Include me now," he insisted, taking a step toward her. A big step.

"I don't think we can manage to be married a year and live in the same house without driving each other crazy." She swallowed, the workings of her throat visible to him. "Or maybe it's just me. But I want you, Gabe. I decided we should enjoy each other, for as long as the marriage lasts."

By the time she finished speaking, he had her in his arms. He intended to tell her how long he wanted the marriage to last. But the minute he touched her, words went out of his head. Except for one.

Bed.

He wanted to find that damn bed quickly, because he knew he wouldn't be able to stand much longer. He swept her into his arms and blindly ran into it as he kissed her senseless. They'd talk later. Now he had to feed the hunger that raged through him.

Memory of the one night they'd shared ten years ago had haunted him. He'd never found another woman to make him feel as Katie had. As he ran his hands over her body, now bare of that X-rated nightgown, he discovered that paradise again.

"Gabe, you have on too many clothes," Katie protested, her fingers working on his shirt. When they reached his belt buckle, he gave up kissing her and helped.

Soon he was as bare as she and their mutual pleasure had him hanging on to his control, wanting Katie to share the pleasure.

Until a frightening thought occurred.

He hadn't brought any condoms with him.

Sort of as a safeguard to his hunger. He figured he wouldn't be tempted to seduce Katie if he knew he had no protection for her.

"Damn! Katie, I didn't bring any condoms! I didn't think—we don't want you to get pregnant!" he exclaimed, even though he prayed she'd tell him she'd welcome his child.

Which, of course, meant he'd be able to make love to her tonight.

"I brought some," she whispered, and motioned to the nightstand where a pile of gold-foil-wrapped packages lay.

He was grateful. Really he was. He wanted to make love to Katie. But there was a sorrow that lessened his pleasure. She was prepared for tonight.

And for leaving him.

He dismissed that thought. He would focus on the here and now. Maybe he could persuade her to give their marriage a chance.

He snatched a packet and prepared himself even as his lips covered hers. She wanted him. That was a start to their future. It would be up to him to convince her.

KATHERINE AWOKE ALONE.

Her hand reached out to the place where Gabe had been. It was cold. She drew his pillow beneath her head and inhaled his scent.

Three times they'd made love last night. Three glorious times of losing herself in him. Of discovering the glory of loving someone in every way possible.

Her eyes filled with tears.

The bedroom door opened and Gabe stared at her. "You're awake? I—what's wrong? Why are you crying?"

Katherine hadn't realized the tears had spilled over onto her cheeks. She hastily scrubbed her cheeks with her hands. "I'm still tired."

He didn't move, and she wasn't surprised. Men didn't like to deal with tears. Sex, yes, but tears, retribution, remorse, no.

But he proved her wrong. Instead of disappearing, he came into the bedroom and shut the door behind him before crossing to the bed and sitting beside her. "Did I hurt you? Are you in pain?"

Oh, yeah. Mortal pain. But not the kind he meant. "No, of course not. You were a wonderful lover."

Her compliment didn't appear to interest him. He studied her, a solemn look on his face. "Katie, we have to talk."

Dread filled her. "I guess I wasn't as competent as the women you're used to. But I'll get better, Gabe. I'll work at it."

He groaned. "Damn, woman, if you get any better, I'll never get out of bed." He bent to kiss her as relief flooded her. The kiss immediately zoomed from lips touching to total involvement.

But before she could start removing his clothes, he pulled back. "No. This time we talk."

"About what?"

"I lied to you."

She frantically tried to think of what he'd told her, but it couldn't have been about the will. After all, Mac had confirmed what Gabe had told her. "About what?"

"About my reason for marrying you. Do you remember my first day back in town? When I was so angry?"

She nodded.

"I was angry because I wasn't indifferent to you."

As a declaration, it was lukewarm, but she found his words encouraging. "You weren't?"

He looked down at his hands, tightly clasped between his knees. "Katie, I married you because I love you, more than I did ten years ago. I don't want to let you go. Ever."

His words were so exactly what she wanted to hear, she was afraid she'd imagined them. "You were very angry."

"Will you forgive me?"

"You were justified. I didn't know what Gran was going to do, but it *was* my fault."

He'd been leaning toward her, reaching for her, but her words stopped him. "How was it your fault?"

"After Darrell was killed, I was over visiting

with Gran and we talked about him. I didn't have anyone to talk to. It all just burst out of me.''

''What burst out of you?''

''How miserable our marriage was. And how guilty I felt. I was honest with Darrell. I told him I didn't love him, but he thought it would be all right. But I didn't tell him I was still in love with you.''

Gabe stared at her. Then he grabbed her shoulders and pulled her toward him. ''You *were* in love with me?''

Hanging her head, she said, ''I still am. But I promise I won't hold you to the marriage. When you've got your inheritance—''

She didn't get to finish her promise. Gabe was kissing the life out of her. Like a starving man before a feast. Several minutes later, they came up for air.

''Dear God, Katie, you mean you've loved me all this time? You loved me when I yelled at you? When I stormed into your shop?''

She nodded.

''Did you hear what I told you? That I love you? That I don't ever want to leave you?''

She reached out a shaking hand to touch his lips. ''Did you really say that? I thought I imagined it.''

He chuckled. ''Let me give you some more to imagine, sweetheart.'' He stood and ripped his clothes off before joining her in bed.

It wasn't long before the moment came to don a condom. But Gabe made no move to do so. Katie was enjoying his activities, but she surfaced long enough to point out his neglect.

He raised his head and stared at her. "Don't you want children?"

"Well, yes, but—" Then, as reality dawned on her, she beamed up at him. "We can have children! Oh, Gabe, yes, I want your baby." She threw her arms around his neck and almost cut off all oxygen.

He kissed her, easing the hold on his neck. "I'll use a condom if you want to wait, but I'm ready. Just like I've been ready for you for the past ten years."

Tears seeped from her closed eyes.

"Katie? Are you all right?"

"Oh, I'm more than all right. I'm the most fortunate woman in the world." She opened her eyes and smiled at him. "You were worth the wait, Gabe Dawson. Definitely worth the wait."

He grinned. "So were you, but there'll be no more waiting around here. We're going to have it all."

Epilogue

Katherine signed the contract for her carrot cake recipe in Alex's office six weeks later. There had been details to work out, and, of course, she'd gone on her honeymoon.

She smiled, thinking about the four days in Colorado Springs. People had asked her if she liked the Rockies. She'd assured them the Rockies were spectacular.

Someday she'd need to go see them.

She'd been much too busy on her honeymoon to pay any attention to a pile of rocks.

"I know it's a good contract," Alex said, staring at her, "but somehow I think you're remembering something about Gabe. That's the look you always get when you talk about him."

Katherine blushed. "You know me too well."

Alex smiled. "Or maybe it's because I've been there, done that…thank goodness."

"Yeah, we're pretty lucky, aren't we?"

"Yes. This town is magic. The next thing you know, you'll be throwing up every morning."

Katherine didn't say anything, but her cheeks burned. The bag at her feet contained a home test she intended to use when she got home.

"Katie Dawson! You're pregnant!"

"I don't know yet. Maybe."

"When are you going to see Samantha?"

"I'm going to take the test today. Then when Gabe gets home, I'll tell him. After that, I'll shout it to the world."

"Oh, that's wonderful! All our babies will be in school together," Alex enthused. "I think Melanie and Spence are working on another one, too."

"Don't say anything to Gabe, please," Katherine pleaded. "I want to surprise him."

Alex assured her she'd keep silent.

GABE LEFT THE OFFICE at two. It was Friday, and he wanted to be home with his wife. She'd cut back on her hours at The Lemon Drop Shop since their return. They spent every minute they could together.

She was in the kitchen when he came through the back door. He didn't hesitate to wrap his arms around her and greet her with a kiss.

When he started walking her toward the door that led to the bedroom, his mouth still on hers, she stopped him.

"Wait."

"What? You don't love me anymore?" His grin, he knew, was big enough for her to know he was kidding. Their weeks of marriage had been absolute paradise.

She slapped his arm. "Silly! You know better. But I have something to tell you."

He nibbled at her mouth, then her throat, losing interest in anything she had to say. He wanted her…as he always did.

"Gabe! You're not paying attention."

"Yes, I am, sweetheart. I'm paying attention to what's important. You're the one still talking."

With a warm chuckle that only increased his ardor, she abruptly agreed. "You're right."

He scooped her into his arms and headed for the bedroom.

An hour later, as they lay in each other's arms, sated, their breathing having returned to normal, he drew lazy circles on her stomach with his finger. "What announcement did you have to make when I got home? Another contract for your cobbler recipe?"

"Oh! I forgot about that. Yes, they're going to pay me the same amount for it as they did for the carrot cake."

"Terrific. I love having a rich wife." His fingers traveled up her body to her breasts.

She grimaced as he stroked her. Frowning, he looked at her. "Did I hurt you?"

"Not really, but you'll need to be a little more careful for a while."

He froze, then he grabbed her, pulling her close. "Something's wrong! Did you go to Samantha? What is it? Do you need to go into the hospital? What can we do?"

That throaty laughter that warmed his soul relieved some of his panic.

"Nothing's wrong. I'll go to Samantha next week. I don't need to go to the hospital yet."

The panic returned. "But you'll have to go to the hospital? Dear God, what's wrong? Tell me!"

"Well, I could stay here, but I don't think you'll want me to."

"Katie, you're killing me! What's wrong?"

"I told you nothing was wrong. But the hospital is better for delivering babies. And I won't have to stay long, just a day or two."

"Oh, good, I—delivering babies?" he thundered, staring at her. When she nodded, he swooped her up into his embrace again.

Minutes later, when he'd asked every conceivable question, kissed her a thousand times, and laughed with heady delight, he said, "If it's a girl, I'd like to name her after Gran. Would you mind?"

"I don't even know Gran's first name. What was it?"

"Rachel."

"I love the name Rachel. We'll name her Rachel Margaret, after Gran and my mother. How about that?"

"I love it. And I love you. And if it's a boy, we can name him…" He paused, considering names.

"How about William Grant? That way he'll have your initials, but he won't have to be called Junior."

Gabe had been named William Gabriel after his father. "That's perfect. Absolutely perfect. Hey, we're good at choosing names. We're going to have to have a lot of kids to fill all the names.''

She grinned. ''Let's take them one at a time, Mr. Dawson. You might be tired of losing your sleep to a screaming baby after just one.''

''One at a time sounds perfect,'' he assured her, kissing her again. ''In fact, everything about our life is perfect, Mrs. Dawson. Absolutely perfect.''

She couldn't agree more.

Judy Christenberry
will return to Harlequin American Romance
this December, contributing to our special
RETURN TO TYLER *in-line continuity.*
Don't miss the fun!

Romance is just one click away!

online book **serials**

➢ *Exclusive* to our web site, get caught up in both the daily and weekly online installments of new romance stories.

➢ Try the Writing Round Robin. Contribute a chapter to a story created by our members. Plus, winners will get prizes.

romantic **travel**

➢ Want to know where the best place to kiss in New York City is, or which restaurant in Los Angeles is the most romantic? Check out our Romantic Hot Spots for the scoop.

➢ Share your travel tips and stories with us on the romantic travel message boards.

romantic reading **library**

➢ Relax as you read our collection of Romantic Poetry.

➢ Take a peek at the Top 10 Most Romantic Lines!

Visit us online at

www.eHarlequin.com
on Women.com Networks

HEUT1

HARLEQUIN

Duets™

Pick up a Harlequin Duets™
from August-October 2000
and receive $1.00 off the
original cover price. *

Experience the "lighter side of love"
in a Harlequin Duets™.
This unbeatable value just became
irresistible with our special introductory
price of $4.99 U.S./$5.99 CAN. for
2 Brand-New, Full-Length
Romantic Comedies.

Offer available for a limited time only.
Offer applicable only to Harlequin Duets™.
*Original cover price is $5.99 U.S./$6.99 CAN.

HDMKD

COMING NEXT MONTH

CNM0900